Ghosts, Witches & Weird Tales of Virginia Beach

Revised Edition

Also by Lillie Gilbert, Belinda Nash, & Deni Norred

Bayside History Trail: A View From the Water
ISBN: 978-0-938423-09-6

Ghosts, Witches & Weird Tales of Virginia Beach

Compiled & written
by
Lillie Gilbert, Belinda Nash,
& Deni Norred

Revised Edition

Eco Images

Virginia Beach, Virginia

Published by:
ECO IMAGES
Virginia Beach, Virginia

ISBN: 978-0-93842-312-6
Revised Edition

Available from:
Bayside Researchers
1428 Back Cove Rd
Virginia Beach, VA 23454

(757) 496-6093

Table of Contents

Chapter 5: We Had Witches ?!?

Chapter 6: Haunts of Private Residences

Foreword

If there are such things as ghosts – we have been arguing about whether or not they exist for the past 4,000 years or so – then why are there so many reported restless spirits in Virginia, which well may be the most haunted state in the country? Parapsychology experts list some possible reasons. In 400 years of history here, there has been much tragedy leading to an unaccountable number of traumatic deaths, which many believe is a leading cause for spectral return. Wars – with the Indians, with the British, and with ourselves (the Civil War) – caused hundreds of thousands of Virginians to die before they were ready.

Then there are the houses. Hans Holzer, who has written more than 100 books on the paranormal, says, "The rolling hills south of Washington, dotted as they are with magnificent manor homes, many of them dating back to colonial days, seem to provide the kind of atmosphere ghosts prefer."

Virginia Beach, one of the most haunted areas in the entire Commonwealth, has an additional reason for its reported preponderance of spirits. It was here, in the early 1930s, that the legendary Edgar Cayce, widely acknowledged as the greatest psychic of modern times, chose to found the Association for Research and Enlightenment – an organization dedicated to physical, mental and spiritual self-improvement programs through researching and applying the information in Cayce's more than 14,000 documented psychic readings.

Why did Cayce choose Virginia Beach? His grandson, Charles Thomas Cayce, says metaphysics entered into the decision. "Virginia Beach was near two large bodies of water, the Chesapeake Bay and the Atlantic Ocean, and he believed the sand of the beach had special energy in it. There was an implication about the energies of the area being particularly conducive to psychic forces," Charles Thomas said.

The sea may also be responsible for one more possible cause for so many lingering apparitions – the coastline of Virginia Beach is littered with tragic shipwrecks and the remains of sailors who never made it through vicious storms to home port.

It should be noted, too, that Virginia Beach was the home of perhaps the most infamous (suspected) witch in American history – Grace Sherwood.

And so, authors Lillie Gilbert, Belinda Nash, and Deni Norred have written a book that chronicles many of the more fascinating ghost and witch traditions of the region. It is an incisive combination that includes both first hand interviews with living witnesses to paranormal activity, and long-held legends that have been passed down through the centuries, generation to generation. It should be pointed out that many experts consider folklore a soft form of history.

And, indeed, the authors have flavored their chapters with historical background on some of the most famous houses and most colorful characters in the city's past. Even if one is not a believer in the supernatural, there is more than sufficient factual information in this book on the parade of people and places in Virginia Beach to warrant a read that will prove enjoyable, entertaining, and educational as well.

L. B. Taylor, Jr.

(Author of many Virginia ghost books)

Words From The Authors

I like the word "Ghost." The word can be said as a whisper...starting softly and slowly. The "o" and "s" can last nearly forever and the sound then disappears with the abrupt phoneme, "t." It's what we imagine as children watching a shadowy or wispy white mist that rises noiselessly up an old staircase, turns a corner, and vanishes. That's what "ghost" sounds like. It is the verbal equivalent of its visual image. It's a poem all by itself.

Long before I thought about the sound of the word "ghost," I was enthralled by what I would later learn was called "paranormal." That word doesn't have quite the ring as "ghost." It doesn't paint a picture. One wonders if things we don't readily understand get lumped into odd categories and filed away for examination when we are more comfortable with them. Ghosts, spirits, or witches seem to make us squirm, the comfort level ranging from disbelief to fear.

...Lillie

Many people envision ghosts as wispy and cloud-like, moaning apparitions, sometimes with sounds of dragging heavy, clanking chains; they may witness the unexplainable movement of objects or hear the slamming of doors as they leave a room. Some of these I have encountered. For example, on a July afternoon in the middle of a heat wave, while walking up the old path from the shore to Ferry Plantation House, where I work as a director, I felt a cold shiver go up my spine. This chill would stop anyone in his or her tracks. It made me ask myself, do I want to venture any farther today? At that moment I could only recall the many stories that others had told me of the unexplained. Had I ventured onto an unmarked grave? Was this spirit making me aware of his or her presence or was my imagination running wild? Had this spirit once been in the courtyard of the 1735 courthouse once near here, or was it of an indentured servant working off his passage, a shackled slave never wanting to leave the plantation and thus roaming on in limbo? Was this the spirit of one who died by accident, or of a diseased child who never had a chance to live out his or her life in the manor house? One day I hope to have the answers to these questions.

With over three hundred years of history being recorded at the site of Ferry Plantation House, we may be stirring up a few intriguing memories. There is much work to do and, even though I hear footsteps overhead on the next floor while I am alone in the house and have felt a presence on the stairs, I will not be frightened off. There is a presence here and I will not offend. I feel if the spirits are kept happy and content they may not mind my presence in the manor house.

...Belinda

Ghosts? I long ago retired both my cartoonish Casper and campfire horror notions of them. Don't get me wrong... I am a believer... but nowadays I am of the opinion, with some degree of sympathy, that "real" specters more often co-exist with rather than "haunt" us. I think ghosts are more the tormented than the tormenters, harmless more than harmful. But then again, my beliefs about ghosts are not research-based and are perhaps naïve, certainly subject to change. I really know so little about ghosts. And witches... weren't yesterday's witches today's intuiters and psychics?

Admittedly, I easily succumb to goose bumps and hair prickles when told a ghost or witch tale. Perhaps oddly, along with such enthrallment rises a feeling of envy towards those who have had ghostly encounters, of whom I am not sure I am one. Ghosts. I wish to some day definitively experience one.

...Deni

Introduction

There still lingers, in those pockets of the mind
where shadows are turned into demons
and where things go bump in the night,
a flutter of the heart when the clock strikes twelve
and a yearning for fire lit hearths where children listen
to ghost stories on long, cold winter nights...
The ghost story is not just a part of history. It is history!

~ Bob Meredith, *The Haunted Cotswolds*, 1999

This book is not an attempt to frighten or try to explain in academic terms the possible explanations for what we are about to tell. We simply offer a collection of odd tales woven with bits of history and Virginia Beach local lore...things to ponder, stories to contemplate, and the intrigue of the unexplained. Are these stories or parts of them true? Are there spirits around us? Are the ghosts and witches real? This may be the time for you to decide. Turn on a light, curl up with your favorite pillow and enjoy.

Acknowledgements

Many thanks to the brave tellers of remembrances and stories of things that have been strange and unexplainable to them. Fielding Tyler and Julie Pouliot, previously of the Old Coast Guard Station Museum, were kind to give time and enthusiasm as well as information, old maps and pictures. Brad Mitchell on his day off from duties at False Cape State Park got permission to drive us to places that we would never have been able to reach. He introduced us to a co-worker who shared a spooky encounter with an unexplained visitor. Nancy Warren and Pat Berson shared their stories about the former Woodhouse Manor. Proofreaders at various stages along the way were Anne Henry (who generously loaned us a wealth of informative source material), Chris Williams, Joe Gilbert and Alice Widman. Barbara Henley put us on the trail of *Stone and Burroughs* and was very encouraging. Barbara Vaughan loaned us the book about *Stone and Burroughs*. Cliff Love was enthusiastic about sharing the names of locals with whom we could speak concerning their experiences with their own haunted houses, although some were unable to allow us to write about these experiences for fear of lowering their property values or the fear of non-spectral intruders who might want to snoop on private property. We agreed not to publish this information. And thanks to Miss Baird, my fourth grade teacher, who gave me (Lillie) my first ghost book.

Chapter 1

Ghosts
of
Shipwrecks

*The sea knows all things,
for at night when the winds are asleep
the stars confide to him their secrets.
In his breast are stored away all the elements
that go to make up the round world.
Beneath…lie buried the sunken kingdoms
of fable and legend…*

~ Elbert Hubbard

The Tragedy Near Little Island

The Surfman's Motto:
You have to go out, but you do not have to come back.

~ Patrick Etheridge, Cape Hatteras Life-Saving Station

ittle Island may be the only Virginia Beach city park with its own resident ghost! The story is tied to the wreck of the German clipper ship, *Elisabeth* or *Elizabeth* (alternate spelling), which left Hamburg, Germany in November 1886 heading for Baltimore. The 1239-ton ship was carrying a cargo of kaninite (manure salt) and 5,000 empty petroleum barrels when it went aground on a sandbar during a brutal northeast wind and snow-storm. The date was January 8, 1887. In the dark early morning hours, "Keeper" Belanga of the Little Island Life-Saving Station was alerted to the dilemma. He assembled his men along with some of those from the Dam Neck Mills Station. He first attempted to land a Breeches Buoy on the ship by means of a Lyle Gun, a special device for firing the line by which passengers could be brought to the shore. The Lyle Gun was used repeatedly to no avail. As the last shot was fired and the connection did not complete the rescue attempt, the surfmen, as the

16

crew was called, and Keeper Belanga regrouped. They then knew that the only way to attempt to save the sailors in their lifeboat was to go to them. The keeper decided to wait for the tide to change, which would allow them to launch the surfboat safely to complete, they thought, the rescue.

Keeper Belanga hand-picked his crew for the dangerous task: himself, Surfmen George Stone, John Land, and Frank Tedford of Little Island Station, and Surfmen John Etheridge, John Spratley, and James Belanga of Dam Neck Mills Station. With the high winds and blowing snow, visibility was extremely limited. The freezing conditions were unbearable and the water temperature must have been bone-chilling. Certainly anyone in this rough Atlantic water would have suffered from hypothermia within several minutes.

Men from both life-saving stations were in a single surfboat on their way to meet destiny. Only after the rescue boat arrived broadside to the *Elisabeth* did those sailors who were still alive leave their ship (Belanga, 2004). With their passengers, the surfmen headed back to the beach. Approaching the shore, suddenly a chilled, powerful breaker capsized the surfboat and it is said to have spun over and over in the surf, all men now in the freezing water (Shanks and York, 1996). One can imagine the helplessness of communication amidst waves and wind: men screaming to be heard, their voices lost to the surf sounds. The outcome of this event was devastating for the surfmen and for the ship's crew. Five surfmen and all twenty-two men from the *Elisabeth* lost their lives (Pouliot, 1986).

Those brave rescuers who gave their lives were Keeper Abel Belanga and his hand-picked crew, one of whom was his brother, James Belanga, and his brothers-in-law John Land, Joseph Spratley, and George Stone (Bennett, 1998). Only two surfmen survived, John Etheridge and Frank Tedford; the latter was another Belanga brother-in-law. With the assistance of another woman, Tedford's wife pulled her collapsed husband back to the station to save his life. The *Elisabeth*, stranded between the two life-saving stations, Dam Neck Mills and Little Island, was battered to pieces in the waves. This event is one of the most tragic shipwrecks to have occurred along the Virginia coast.

Marshall Belanga, one of only four remaining men of the Belanga family whose roots in this area trace back to the 1700s, maintains that the wreck of the *Elisabeth* lies about 200 yards off the beach. He relayed (2004), "I've sat on my boat directly above that wreck many a time and looked down onto that gantry." He paused, shook his head slowly, and continued, "Looking down, you can just imagine what it must have been like for those men during that storm."

Brothers Marshall and Marvin Belanga

Gravemarkers of (top to bottom) Abel Belanga, James Belanga, and John Spratley

He lost his life at the wreck of the German Ship Elizabeth while trying to rescue the sailors from a Watery grave.

~ Inscription on tombstone of Abel Belanga, born Sept. 13, 1842, died Jan. 8, 1887

Several claim to have heard the ghost of brave Keeper Belanga in the park office, which is actually located in a building that Abel Belanga could never have entered. Built in 1925, it is in a different location and 38 years after the Belanga family tragedy and the loss of the *Elisabeth*. Descendant Marshall Belanga (2004) said he has heard stories of ghosts there, but cannot confirm their validity. He did add, however, "This is not to say that I don't believe someone from the past can't come tapping on your shoulder one day."

One park employee believes there may be more than one ghost in the building, and they are "nice" ones. He has had no problems with them when he has spent time in the office alone. When he arrives, he always makes sure to say, "Good morning, guys," and when leaving, "Goodnight; keep the house safe, guys. See you tomorrow." Perhaps Keeper Belanga and his surfmen's enduring devotion to service has caused the area to be bathed in their benevolence.

Following its construction, the older building, the 1876 station, was used for boat and rescue equipment storage. Keeper Belanga and his co-workers would have used the gear from this building in their last rescue attempt of 1887. The entire building was lost to the sea in the major hurricane that washed away much of the Little Island community on August 23, 1933, including the 1876 station building that housed the equipment used by the men of the U.S. Life Saving Service. It was in the 1925 building that most of the residents of Little Island sought shelter from the storms of 1933. They had to endure two hurricanes that year, the second one just 24 days after the devastating August

storm. The sturdy U.S. Coast Guard Station of Little Islar
these storms and many more. Bridging an important hi
the building is still in use today serving the citizens of Virg..
as the park's recreational office.

To its honor, on March 15, 2001, the Virginia Beach Historical
Review Board officially recognized the remaining buildings of the
Little Island Coast Guard Station as a place of local historical
importance. The complex of buildings is now part of the Virginia
Beach Historical Register.

Shipwreck

by R. S. Chilton

A long, low reach of level sand,
Packed erewhile by the maddened waves
As the storm-wind drove them toward the land:
A boat on the shore and nothing more
To tell of the dead who sank to their graves,
To the sound of the wild sea's roar.

The ship went down at night, they say,
Wrestling with wind and wave to the last,
Like a great sea-monster fighting at bay:
The fisherman tells how he heard the bells
Ring in the lulls of the pitiless blast,
Mingled with wild farewells.

The winds are asleep, and the sea is still—
Still as the wrecked beneath its waves,
Dreamless of all life's good or ill:
A boat on the shore and nothing more
Tells of the dead who sank to their graves,
To the sound of the wild sea's roar.

Ghost Surfman of the Old Coast Guard Station

We shall not know the ships that lie
Deep sunk upon their shifting floors
Nor whose the ghosts that flit and fly
Upon their thousand-sided shores.

~ J.F. Dahlgren

he Old Coast Guard Station at Virginia Beach's oceanfront has a ghost story of its own. It is said to be the haunt of John Woodhouse Sparrow, "ghost surfman" of the century-old decommissioned building formerly called Seatack Lifesaving Station. By at least 1902 the building became known as the Virginia Beach Life-Saving Station.

Sparrow was a heroic figure in the infamous December 21, 1900 wreck of the *Jennie Hall*, a three-masted schooner from Maine carrying asphalt (Evans-Hylton, 2003). He was a surfman, one of the crew from two life-saving stations that set out by surfboat to assist the *Jennie Hall*. This venture was more successful than that of the *Elisabeth* for both the rescuers and rescued: five of the eight men aboard the schooner were saved and no surfman perished (United States Coast Guard, 2001). Although a large wave washed Sparrow overboard the surfboat, he remarkably surfaced about 50 feet away, and was pulled in and aboard by a safety line thrown to him by his loyal fellow surfmen (Pouliot, 1986). Undaunted by this incredible escape from death, he remained on the staff of the station.

John Sparrow died in 1935 after thirty-three years of service as a surfman (Mansfield, 1989). Perhaps in reference to the white draft horses the surfmen had used to haul carts of lifesaving equipment (Ruegsegger, 2003), his last words were reported to be, "Can you see that great white horse coming through the window?" (Tyler, 2004).

It may be the specter of Sparrow whom a number of people have reportedly spotted through the museum's windows in its off hours, prompting them to report to the police a suspected burglary in progress. Among their many visits to investigate the place, not once have the police  confirmed a break-in. Was it Sparrow who passed through one museum employee as a rush of cold air as she climbed the stairs to the old watch tower one hot summer day? And was it the surfman's specter that was spotted by another staff member in the lower gallery? When this employee approached to advise him that it was nearly closing time, the man, dressed in clothes of an earlier era, vanished before her eyes. Sparrow's spirit may also be the culprit who occasionally turns the pages of the old seaman's logbook kept under glass at the museum (Ruegsegger, 2003).

Misty Neal and her mother were among many who have taken the tour at the Old Coast Guard Station. Standing side-by-side, the two were listening to the tour guide talk about rescue efforts and such, her mother to Misty's right. Captivated by the lecture, Misty was suddenly distracted by a distinct presence to her right. "It felt like my entire right side was dipped in cold electricity," she explained. The feeling was so intense that it distracted her entirely from the tour guide's lecture. As soon as the two left the building, she and her mother simultaneously started jabbering about the "presence," her mother, of course, having felt its coldness to her left. Misty sensed it was a male, seemingly standing there listening to the

talk about Lyle Guns and whatnot, making sure the tour guide "knew his stuff." Once satisfied, the fellow "strolled" off somewhere else!

But then again, there is reason to speculate that besides Sparrow, others also long since gone are roaming the museum in their unrest. Of course, not all of the surfmen's brave and dangerous ventures ended as did the shipwrecked *Jennie Hall*, with few or no deaths to tally. After a shipwreck the bodies of the sea's victims were often stored in the

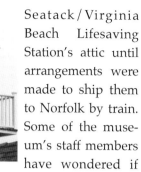

Seatack / Virginia Beach Lifesaving Station's attic until arrangements were made to ship them to Norfolk by train. Some of the museum's staff members have wondered if the poor souls of these stashed corpses could be responsible for the reported hauntings through the years.

The Old Coast Guard Station is located at 24th Street and the Boardwalk, Virginia Beach, Virginia. It is housed in the former United States Coast Guard Station / Virginia Beach Life-Saving Service building. The structure is listed as a Virginia Historic Landmark on the National Register of Historic Places. The museum exhibits portray the history of the U.S. Life-Saving / U.S. Coast Guard Service and stories of heroic shipwreck rescues by members of the service.

The museum offers a research library, archives, educational programs, a museum shop, guided tours, and other services. There is a charge for admission. The Museum Store may be visited without charge. Contact the staff at (757) 422-1587 or on the web at www.old coastguardstation.com for hours of operation and other information.

Although it has been slightly moved and turned (the side with the doors for surfboats originally faced the ocean), the building is intact. One of the interesting modern features of the museum is the TowerCam mounted atop the building. This computer-assisted scope allows for a view of the boardwalk and the Atlantic Ocean as it appears from the prominent old lookout tower. Web users are able to view the life around the oceanfront. Like the keepers and surfmen of the past (and perhaps Sparrow, to this day), this scope is ever watchful of the ocean's conditions.

The Cape Henry Light

Wild, wild the storm, and the sea high running,
Steady the roar of the gale, with incessant undertone muttering...
Waves, air, midnight, their savagest trinity lashing...
Out in the shadows their milk-white combs careering...
Where through the murk the easterly death-wind breasting,
Through cutting swirl and spray watchful and firm advancing,
(That in the distance! is that a wreck? is the red signal flaring?)
A group of dim, weird forms, struggling, the night confronting,
That savage trinity warily watching.

~ Walt Whitman, *Patroling Barnegat*

ere you ever told the story of the ghost of Cape Henry Lighthouse? Here it is, as written by Alexander Crosby Brown in his book, *Chesapeake Landfalls* (1974).

It's been so long now than no one alive could possibly remember, but it was about a hundred years ago that the little brig HATTIE BELLE came to grief at the entrance to Chesapeake Bay not far from where the light-house itself stands. Many witnesses swore that that night the light was out. But all agreed, with the hurricane sweeping in from the sea, the HATTIE BELLE was a goner anyway, light or no light.

Cape Henry's keeper, poor old Jeremiah [Jeb] Thatcher, just loved his lighthouse and he kept its new Fresnel lenses sparkling bright, never failing to see that the clockwork turning gears were working properly and that enough oil was on hand. This was quite a job for a retired mariner with a game leg, for everyday the oil had to be toted up the hundred odd circular steps to the lamp room at the top of the tower.

They say that it's Captain Jeb's ghost who comes back to haunt the place. One thing that had gotten under Jeb's skin was the decision announced by the Lighthouse Board in 1872 that the then eighty-year-old tower was in danger of falling down and must be replaced. Old Jeb knew it was strong enough to stand any weather, but they wouldn't believe him. He was right, of course, for the tower still stands and it's getting on to being 200 years old. [Authors' Note: at the time of this publication (2012), the old lighthouse is 220 years old].

Anyway in 1879 they started building the new Cape Henry Light and it showed its first beams from the 150-foot iron tower on Dec. 15, 1881. Then they closed down the old sandstone lighthouse which George Washington himself had authorized and took out the lamps and reflectors for the new light, suggesting that the god of storms could now go ahead and knock it down any time he had a mind to and no matter. As everyone knows, today the old lighthouse is a National Monument, well cared for by the Association for the Preservation of Virginia Antiquities.

Old Jeb was dead by the time the new lighthouse was built, which is just as well for no one would have listened to him anyway. They said, though, that it was the decision to abandon the old lighthouse that first drove him to drinking a little more than he should. Anyone who knew Lucy Thatcher would not have been entirely in agreement with that, however. No doubt but she hen-pecked her poor husband almost out of reason. And if he began showing up at the Pleasure House Tavern near Lynnhaven with increasing frequency, well, heck! Who could blame him! Anyway, he always left in plenty of time to get back to Cape Henry and get the light lit before sundown.

And so it was on that late September day in 1872, only three months after the Board had announced its plan to build a new lighthouse. This was long before there were any hurricane warning systems and the naming of the storms after dear little girls and, though the weather had been fickle all morning with gusty winds out of the northwest, no one suspected that a hurricane was coming until it was right there. By noon, with Captain Jeb ensconced on his favorite stool at the Pleasure House and hardly in a position there to follow the vagaries of the weather, the wind suddenly veered around to the north, nor-east and commenced to blow a regular muzzler. The moon was coming to the full that night and, combined with the wind, tides had already begun running three to four feet above normal. Even then, there was some flooding along the coast road and the high water was still four hours off. By contrast, it was comfortable and warm in the tavern, else Jeb would have sized up the situation earlier and started on back to be on time to tend to his light.

Meanwhile, the poor little brig HATTIE BELL was slogging it out in the open Atlantic making heavy weather coming down the coast. Her captain hoped as conditions worsened that before too long, he'd be able to make Chesapeake Bay entrance and find a reasonably safe anchorage in Lynnhaven Roads where he could ride out the mounting storm. He was comforted by the fact that, although visibility was badly reduced by mist and flying scud, even after dark the gleam of Cape Henry's powerful light would give him the bearing in time to swing in to safety before fouling himself on Middle Ground Shoals or the lee shore of the cape itself. Meanwhile, all he could do was try to hold his course and pray.

When at length Jeb had downed his last schooner of ale, pushed back from the bar and started out to head for home, he realized right away that, with conditions as they were, he would at best be cutting pretty fine his chances of getting the light lit before early darkness set in. But, as he hurried along at his best game-leg speed, he was soon horrified to discover many places along the road were under water and the tide still not fully in flood. And when, at length, he reached Broad Creek and found the bridge submerged, he knew he would have to take a long detour around by the head of the creek. In his now desperate haste, Jeb frequently slipped and fell, cursing the Lighthouse Board, the weather, and Lucy all in the same breath. In the approaching darkness, he missed the turn among the dunes, losing many more irreplaceable minutes. Now he realized he'd never get to the lighthouse in time. Crying out in agony, he sank to his knees and pounded his fists on the ground. In a minute he was up again and propelled by the wind, he slogged on toward the cape.

With the mounting wind and sea, visibility on the brig close to the water was now down to a matter of yards. Still, the HATTIE BELLE'S skipper did not despair, realizing that soon the protective gleam of the lighthouse would cut through the murk and point his way in to a safe haven. It had to. He did not realize, though, that even then treacherous currents were sweeping his frail craft closer to outlying shoals. It was now almost completely dark. Where was the guiding light? Surely it would show up now! Could they be that far off in the reckoning?

Time passed, the seas were beginning to break and stinging spray hurled from the foaming wave crests all but blinded the straining helmsman. And then, without a moment's warning it happened. The HATTIE BELLE gave a desperate lurch as her keel crashed onto the shoaling bottom. Her back broken and with garboard planks stove and water pouring in, the little vessel immediately broached to. Then the foremast snapped clean off and a tangle of rigging falling overside dragged the other mast with it and forced the stricken vessel down on her beam ends. Breakers were everywhere. Those men on deck were swept off into the maelstrom. Those below drowned like rats in a hole. Not one soul lived to tell the tale.

By the time Captain Jeb reached Cape Henry and climbed up his hundred steps to light the lantern, the doomed HATTIE BELLE had been swept hard and fast on the sandy shore even within sight of the tower. Rescuers quickly gathered on the beach, but there was nothing that could be done. Even if a boat could have been launched through the surf, it was obvious there were no survivors left on the HATTIE BELLE to bring ashore.

With the light going, old Jeb climbed down from his tower and joined the knot of men looking seaward to the tortured wreck being flung like a chip amongst the breakers. Beside himself in agony he cried out and pushing the others aside, he strode down into the water. Then he flung himself into the waves in a last desperate attempt to get out to lend aid to the poor wretches of the HATTIE BELLE. The rescuers yelled and tried to stop this suicidal attempt, but to no avail. On he went until he, too, was smothered by the raging seas, his mercy mission doomed from the very start.

Next day the bodies washed ashore half a mile down the beach – all ten men of the crew of the HATTIE BELLE plus the lighthouse keeper of Cape Henry Light – all gone to glory.

It was some years afterwards, when a new keeper had been appointed to care for the new lighthouse and the old Cape Henry tower stood abandoned and forlorn with broken windows in the empty lamp room providing a refuge for storm-tossed sea birds, that local residents began to notice with astonishment that sometimes, on particularly evil nights, a light seemed to shine forth from the old tower. And some noticed, as well, putting two and two together, that on the anniversary of the wrecking of the HATTIE BELLE, in addition to the light, supernatural wails seemed to emanate from the tower. Shivering, they said that it must be the restless ghost of old Captain Jeb returned to tend the light that failed on that stormy night the HATTIE BELLE came to grief.

How can this possibly be true, you say? The lighthouse has had no means of illumination for nigh on 90 years. Yet, on these occasions, its powerful beams still seem to shine seaward hoping to guide a ghostly brig to a safe haven within the Capes. {Authors' Note: The lighthouse *has not been illuminated for over 130 years!}*

I have seen that very light with my own eyes. Yes, and even taken a photograph of it, too!

Now do you believe the story of the ghost of Cape Henry?

Actually, it's hard to believe and I'm glad that I don't have to try, for, after all, I just finished making it all up myself. I needed a story to go with that photograph! For the light I saw from the lofty tower was merely the sun lined up behind it so that its rays shone through the empty panes. Captain Jeb – rest in peace!

~ Reprinted courtesy of Norfolk County
Historical Society of Chesapeake.

The Fire Keepers

Before the advent of lighthouses, fires were used as an earlier method of lighting harbor entrances to guide ships along the Atlantic and on the Chesapeake Bay. At Cape Henry, the fire's "keeper" gathered pine knots in the surrounding sandy "desert" and burned these in a large metal basket. Keepers of fire beacons were subject to danger posed by flame-snuffing pirates who stood to profit from a pitch-black shore. Some pirates, rather than apprehending the fires that assisted colonial navigation, resorted to luring merchant ships through trickery, by lighting their own fires. So important to colonists were these legitimate guiding fires that they organized lookouts to patrol beaches for pirate activity between Lynnhaven River and Cape Henry (Vojtech, 1996).

The original Cape Henry Lighthouse is the first public works project that was authorized by the United States Congress. It had its origins in colonial times, having been proposed as early as 1721 by Governor Alexander Spotswood. By the time money and arrangements were made to begin construction, it was 1774. Tons of stone were delivered to the site at Cape Henry and preliminary foundation stones were laid. By 1775, with no funds and the war with England looming, all work ceased. In 1789, the Commonwealth of Virginia gave two acres of land to the federal government, provided that a lighthouse would be constructed in two years. In 1790, during the second year of George Washington's administration, Congress approved money for the lighthouse at Cape Henry. Work began in 1791 with some of the salvaged stone left by the colonial project and additional stone was brought to the site. The sandstone used to build it is the same that was used at Mt. Vernon, the Capitol and the White House, all quarried in Aquia, Virginia.

With the project completed in October of 1792, the first keeper, appointed by President George Washington, himself, touched flame to wick and the whale oil lamps burned brightly. The original Cape Henry Light is a brick octagonal structure built on the tallest sand dune where the Atlantic Ocean meets the Chesapeake Bay. Local rebels destroyed the original Fresnel lens during the Civil War to make entering the Chesapeake more difficult for Northern troops.

The original Cape Henry Lighthouse is owned and maintained by The Association for the Preservation of Virginia Antiquities (APVA). This organization was founded in 1889 for the specific purpose of preserving historic sites. The Old Cape Henry Lighthouse serves as the official symbol for the City of Virginia Beach. The lighthouse may be visited year-round. Call for hours of operation and current admission fees, (757) 422-9421.

Captain Jorgensen and the Norwegian Lady

Cast your eyes on the
ocean
cast your soul to the sea.
When the dark night
seems endless
Please remember me.

~ Loreena McKennitt

t 25th Street and the Oceanfront stands the bronze Norwegian Lady statue in commemoration of the catastrophic 1891 shipwreck of the Norwegian bark, the *Dictator*. She is a replacement of the ship's figurehead,

1258. Princess Anne Hotel, Va. Beach, Va.

which washed ashore after the wreck and was spotted one day later, bobbing in the surf. The wooden figurehead long stood at 16th Street and Oceanfront before it was removed in 1953, as it had become weathered and eroded (Foss, 2002). Citizens of Moss, Norway presented one of two identical bronze sculptures to Virginia Beach to replace the figurehead. The bronze statue looks out over the Atlantic Ocean near the location of the fatal event and toward her "sister" statue in Norway.

Much to their horror, local residents and guests of the now long-gone original Princess Anne Hotel witnessed in full view the sinking of the *Dictator*. Captain Jorgen Martinius Jorgensen survived but his wife and four-year-old son were among those taken by the rough, relentless sea. Local legend has it that Captain Jorgensen returned to Virginia Beach, Virginia annually on March 27, the anniversary of the tragic event, where at the figurehead he "knelt in the sand in silent prayer, placed red roses at the foot of the figurehead, then cast a bouquet of flowers into the sea" (Foss, 2002). While in reality Jorgensen only came to Hampton Roads one known time after the tragedy, legends of his once-a-year tribute at the Norwegian Lady persisted past his death and segued into tales of the inconsolable captain's ghostly annual appearance (Parker, 2003). A prominent Norfolk citizen of Norwegian descendant donated gravesites in Norfolk's Elmwood Cemetery to Johanna Paulina and Carl Zealand Jorgensen, the Captain's beloved wife and son, respectively.

Figureheads

According to the research of Lawrence Mahan, captain of a "modified replica" of a 1767 Boston Schooner, figureheads were originally placed on ships' bows as "idols to ward off evil spirits and pacify the demons of the sea" (2003). Later they performed different tasks. His summary of the history of figureheads is as follows:

> *Superstitious seafaring people have always sought good luck. Ever since the first vessels were built, sailors trying to ensure safe passage have attempted to pacify mysterious and unpredictable gods with offerings or symbols of faith. The ship's figurehead, a typical example of this tradition, can take many forms, and over the centuries many motifs and symbols have been used for figureheads, including lions, human figures, horses (some with two heads), serpents, doves, geese, as well as imaginary figures such as unicorns, griffins, dragons, and even a Cimbrian bull. Early Viking ships proudly displayed serpents and other deities to ward off evil omens of the deep, while a common figurehead for the American ships was the lion, following the practice of the English ships. But by the middle of the eighteenth century, stylized carvings came into fashion, and a variety of subjects became acceptable subjects for figureheads. A New England vessel displaying a horse's head was sighted at Dunkirk, England in 1744, and soon many boats on both sides of the Atlantic abandoned the standard lion in favor of other figures. Human figures began to appear in the late 1770s. It wasn't long before female figures began to appear. They were used on a great number of commercial ships after 1800, and often ship owners' wives were used as models. Figureheads...became the symbols of individualism and a means of identification.*

Chapter 2

Ghosts of Bases & Stations:

They Didn't Go Home After Their Shifts

… all watches must have an end …
Sometime far in the late hour, when the moon is high
and small above a sea of glittering white,
you will return to the four walls of your room
to drift into dreamless sleep…
through the dying hush of breaking waves
rolling up over consciousness like the foam of a rising tide.

~ E.M. Eller, 1931

The Mischievous Spirit of Seatack Fire Station

Is there within the bounds of nature, perceptible to mortal sense, the reality of what is intended by the word "ghost?" Or is all reputed ghost-seeing pure hallucination on the part of the seer?

~ Frederick H. Hedge, 1881

oday's Seatack Volunteer Fire Department station off Birdneck Road replaced the old wooden fire station housed in what once was Seatack Elementary School. The school deeded the property to the fire department in 1951 (Grube, 1994). This old station is said to have had a resident ghost. "Irving," as he was fondly called by the firefighters, was supposedly named after one of the station's founding members. "Eerie Irving" is said to have caused the stairs to creak, turned on fire engine lights and sirens, slammed doors, and even changed television channels (Dougherty, 1990).

Captain Dan Fentress, formerly assigned to the newer Seatack station built in 1983, heard sounds in the previous station that may or may not be attributed to those typical of an aging building. Whenever anything went awry or couldn't be found, said Fentress, the men would jokingly say, "Well, old Irving's been around again." He recalls that one fellow firefighter once reported seeing wet footsteps on the stairs. Fentress himself took a picture of the station with a blur on it that he refers to as Irving, although he admits it may be attributed to natural aberrations of the developing process. But who knows? Maybe not.

To the dismay of some, the mischievous spirit disappeared when the old wooden building was demolished in 1983. He apparently did not resurface in Seatack's new station.

One may wonder how Seatack station and the Seatack area were named. Sailing ships at sea sometimes had to tack away from the shore in order to make the moves necessary to avoid shoals along the beachfront. To enter or exit the Chesapeake Bay, Virginia Beach was probably the last tack. This "tack to seaward" or sea tack is a probable account for the name.

Dam Neck Naval Ghost

And like a passing thought,
she fled In light away.

~ Robert Burns, *The Vision*

 strange sighting supposedly took place early one morning in December of 1999 at Oceana Naval Base, Dam Neck Annex in the "finger barracks" off the galley, on the bottom floor of the women's wing. As the story goes, a transparent naked slender woman with dark, straight black hair walked right past a sailor showering in the open bays. The alleged apparition emerged from a wall and exited through the hallway door (Carlson & Juliano, 2002).

Dam Neck has an interesting and diverse history. Because of references to dams as markers on old land deeds of the vicinity, it has been hypothesized that the name referred to beaver dams that long ago characterized the area. Perhaps though, the beaver dam theory does not hold water as beavers, trees and salt water do not mix well. The "Neck" would have come from homeland England's common usage of the term as a piece of land surrounded by bays and creeks. As far back as 1780, the area was well known for its mills, which would grind corn and grains into meal and flour (virginiabeachon-line, 1999-2003). The original Dam Neck Mills Life-Saving Station is dated around 1874; it became inactive in 1938 (United States Coast Guard, 2001). During World War II, the United States Navy purchased the property at Dam Neck and built a training center. Today the military base at Dam Neck is located where the lifesaving station once stood (virginiabeachon-line, 1999-2003).

Ghost Stories from Fort Story

Thin, airy shoals of visionary ghosts.

~ Homer, *The Odyssey*

he Cape Henry seascape with its stretches of sand and dunes dotted with beach grass, sea oats and, moving inland from the shoreline, scrubby to tall pines and cedar, has seen human activity, war and strife for eons. The sands were the stomping grounds of Coastal Algonquin Indians who pre-date European contact by thousands of years. We know that in 1607, it was from Cape Henry's dunes that the natives attacked an English expedition's landing party when they came ashore. Later, the area was the setting for much of the action of the Revolutionary War; many a battle was fought at sea just off the cape. In the 1700s the grounds were chosen as the site for a federal lighthouse, the first in the history of our then new nation, for the use and advantage of ships in the vicinity of Virginia's capes. Fort Story at Cape Henry, named for Virginia-born General John P. Story, has been an active military facility since President William Howard Taft in 1913 signed an appropriations bill to purchase the land. Its varied terrain has and continues to be exceptional training grounds (*The Beach*, 1996).

With Cape Henry and its history as the setting, it is no wonder that Fort Story has its share of ghost stories. Some tales are of specters of soldiers who, for some reason, do not formally realize their discharge ... from life, that is. Other sightings and encounters, however, are not of men of the military. Read on.

Gleaned from internet lore are claims that soldiers patrolling the base on cold, wet nights have sighted a mysterious ghostly being along Coast Artillery Road. This apparition allegedly disappears into

the wetlands of the area. It has been said that this may be the ghost of a soldier who was stationed at Fort Story who a few years back committed suicide by hanging himself (The Shadowlands, 2004).

Christina, a young lady now out of the army, shared a few accounts of strange events she personally experienced when stationed at Fort Story a few years back. The following took place in a male barracks in July of 2003 (names have been changed):

> *My friend Tillerman had always claimed he had a ghost in his second floor room of the 119th Barracks. But, he also always advised me not to be afraid of her. When I was playing on Tillerman's game system one day, he and another friend of mine, Kilmer, left to go downstairs to the chow hall. They said they would be right back, at which time Kilmer and I were to go home. I was not alone: Tillerman's roommate was on his bed behind me.*
>
> *I was playing the game system when all of a sudden the TV went off, the alarm clock came on, and the door to the room FLEW open with a loud CRASH. I turned the TV back on and went back to my game-playing. I didn't touch the alarm clock. Tillerman's roommate just sat up, scared. Not even ten seconds later, I heard the hall door open and Tillerman and Kilmer's voices outside. When they returned to the room, I told Tillerman I didn't think his ghost liked me. And, I added, I thought it was time for me to go.*

> *Tillerman was in that room for three years. He always liked to play rap music. After he and his roommate left, two new soldiers moved in. They liked all kinds of music but whenever they tried to play rap, the radio would turn off all by itself. When I told Tillerman about that, he just laughed.*

Barracks are not the only buildings at Fort Story Christina believed to be haunted. She maintains the library on base also had its ghosts. Its off-hours patrons, however, were definitely not former military personnel:

> *I always had to go to first morning formation at 6:15. After formation, I would go to the library. But as it didn't open until 11, I would sleep in back on the couches as I waited. Well, I would always hear these footsteps that sounded like kids running around, which was weird because I knew I was the only one there. I would also hear the loud squeak of the door opening and closing. These noises used to scare me but, as I heard them every day, after awhile I got used to them. Then one day when I was lying down with my eyes closed I heard the hushed voice of a little girl say, "Let's wake her up." I then heard another little girl answer, "Huh huh." I was scared out of my mind… my heart was racing and I didn't open my eyes for at least half an hour, terrified that if I did, I might see two little ghosts!*

Apparently, little girl ghosts were not confined to the library. Christina heard from a male friend of hers who was also stationed at Fort Story that the ghost of a little girl appeared and spoke to him in the family housing barracks. This same man claimed witnessing on many an occasion a guy with his head chopped almost all the way off. Despite his gruesome circumstances, the unfortunate soul always smiled and waved pleasantly at Christina's acquaintance as he was passing. According to another female soldier, ghosts who hid in the bushes near the newer lighthouse at Fort Story sometimes came out and walked behind her; this woman told Christina she always heard their footsteps. She avoided the area whenever possible. Christina's last recounted ghost experience took place in a female barracks:

My drill sergeant often told me that there was a ghost in the female barracks and "it" turned on the water in the shower. As there is no way to turn the spigot off without getting soaked, I guess this particular ghost got a kick out of seeing the drill sergeants get wet. One day when the water in the shower was on, my drill sergeant didn't feel like getting wet yet again. So, he told me to cut the water off. So I went in the shower and got soaked turning it off. He was right, there really was no way at all to turn it off without getting really wet. While I was there I told the ghost, "If you need help at all in any way you give me a sign and I'll help you." I went back to my fire guard in the AIT barracks, which are connected to the female barracks, and I found two girls sleeping on my floor. When I asked them why they were there, they said they saw a ghost running around in the barracks and they didn't want to stay there. The drill sergeant never told these girls about ghosts; in fact, he had just sworn to them there were none, even after he'd just told me about the shower ghost. Not even a few hours later, the electricity went out as far as I could see. The fire alarm went off too and it couldn't be turned off for hours. Now, you can tell me that could have just been coincidence but all I know, I was scared out of my mind, thinking that shower ghost was giving me a "sign"… a BIG one. I acted so weird that my drill sergeant swore he was never going to be on that duty with me again!

Spooks aside, Fort Story at Cape Henry is a must visit for those interested in local history. On its premises for today's visitors are the Cape Henry Memorial Cross, erected in 1935 to mark the place where Jamestown settlers first arrived in 1607, and the two Cape Henry lighthouses, the earliest one built in 1792 as the first to be authorized by the federal government.

Chapter 3

Bizarre Business Events

There are more guests at the table than the hosts invited,
The illuminated hall
Is thronged with quiet, inoffensive ghosts,
As silent as the pictures on the wall.

~ Henry Wadsworth Longfellow, *Haunted Houses*

Cavalier Hotel Tales

We meet them at the doorway, on the stair,
Along the passageways they come and go,
Impalpable impressions on the air,
A sense of something moving to and fro.

~ Henry Wadsworth Longfellow, *Haunted Houses*

amed after the later and more elite colonists of the "traditional times in old Virginia" the word "cavalier" evokes (Mansfield, 1989), this grand eight-story resort hotel was built on a giant sand dune overlooking the Atlantic Ocean. Constructed in an elegant style at a cost of two million dollars, it opened its doors to guests in 1927 and catered to the upper echelon: wealthy and well-known actors and actresses, authors and sports figures, dignitaries and statesmen, politicians and Presidents (Ruehlmann, 1981). During The Cavalier's heyday from the 1930s through 1941, it boasted a reputation as the largest employer of big bands in the world (Rutherford, 2002). The famous, smartly-dressed guests flocked to the facility to dine, dance, golf, sunbathe under oceanfront cabanas, ride horses, play tennis, and swim in the indoor salt-water pool. A top-notch staff of hundreds attended them.

During World War II, the Navy took possession of the hotel and utilized it as a high security radar training facility. It was left in ill repair and after the war The Cavalier's days of splendor appeared to be gone forever. The old hotel closed in 1973 and its contents were sold at public auction. Attention was diverted to the hotel's newer counterpart, the Cavalier Oceanfront, which opened the same year the older hotel was closed. Many wondered whether The Cavalier on the Hill, which now sat vacant, would ever make a comeback.

Fortunately, Gene Dixon, Jr., son of the hotel's former owner, appreciated the architectural and historical gem, purchased the place and resurrected the phoenix from its ashes. He was determined that

the Queen of the beach be restored to her former glory (Ruehlmann, 1981). The Cavalier on the Hill was reopened on a part-time basis in 1976 (Mansfield, 1989). The hotel is now open on a regular basis. Preservation and renovation are ongoing as rooms are enlarged from their original sizes and amenities are modernized (Wacker, 2003).

Personal accounts of ghost encounters are often submitted to internet sites: one local fellow who worked various jobs at the Cavalier Hotel during its years of renovation shared his one and only paranormal encounter there. He was finishing up some demolition work on the third floor, one of six floors out of service for renovation. It was 4:00 in the afternoon. His boss asked him to check out a few of the rooms for their readiness for new carpet. The fellow was alone on the third floor. He entered one room that was stripped of everything and ready for construction. To his left was a piece of plywood leaning against the wall, a sheet draped over it. No big deal; he noticed but didn't think twice about it as he turned right into the bathroom. Looking up, the worker saw that the bathroom's damaged ceiling had been removed. Some of its debris remained on the floor, and he remembered thinking that he needed to clean it up before starting work the next day. His back was to the bathroom door. When he turned around to exit the bathroom, his heart rose to his throat instantly: the piece of plywood he had taken note of in the bedroom was now propped up against and blocking the bathroom door directly in front of him! In a panic, he pushed the plywood down, ran over it and out of the room, ran down the hall, down the stairs, and out of the hotel. Outside at his car before leaving, he stood breathlessly for a moment, looking back at the hotel. "I think I told a few people about my experience, but who's going to believe that story??? IT HAPPENED," he insists.

Modernization of The Cavalier on the Hill apparently has not banished old ghosts from the premises. Although reports are unsubstantiated, locals and visitors tell unusual stories about the grand old hotel. Towels have mysteriously changed color when some guests have reentered their rooms. When these guests, assuming superior service, have complimented staff for changing even unused towels, they have been astonished when told housekeeping had not attended their rooms.

One floor is reported to be home to many ghosts, as manifested by strange noises and whispering voices. The old uniformed gentleman who has ushered many a guest to a particular floor warns that it may be haunted, and suggests the guest may want to request a room on a different floor. When reported to the management that this gentleman inferred the hotel was haunted, it is said the staff routinely maintain his description matches no one working there. In fact, the described hotel uniform the old fellow was wearing seemed reminiscent of an earlier era.

There is another elusive being "seen" at the Cavalier, this one not human ... Several guests have called the front desk to report a cat roaming the halls. Hotel staff members searching halls and stairways have yet to catch a cat. Each perturbed guest, adamant that a cat was on the floor, has been quite indignant that these searches have uncovered ... nothing.

Ghosts are often associated with trauma and at least one tragedy has occurred at the hotel. At age eighty-three, Adolph Coors, the founder of Coors Brewery, had gone to the Cavalier Hotel in Virginia Beach, VA to recover from the flu. On June 5, 1929, the unhappy man met his death at the grand hotel. While *The New York Times* (1929) reported that he "died suddenly of heart disease... as he was dressing for the day," it was no secret locally that the man had mysteriously fallen to his death from a sixth floor window (Virginian-Pilot, 1929). That his will stipulated his Cavalier bill of $1,876.51 be paid in full (Baum, 2001) leaves one to wonder if he knew his days were soon to end.

Adolph Coors was born in 1847 in Germany, at that time known as Prussia, where he was apprenticed to a brewmeister. He brought his talents to the United States and began what was to become the Coors Brewing Company in Colorado. In the Golden, Colorado census of 1880, his occupation is listed was "brewery proprietor." By 1890, he was a millionaire (Baum, 2001).

Coors had retired from brewmaking a full year before a national ban on beer, wine, and spirits. Having diversified to the production of cement, malted milk, and chemical porcelain during Prohibition, he remained financially well off, but chronically unhappy with his beloved brewery gone. He finally turned over the business to his son, Adolph Jr., in 1923 (Baum, 2001).

The historic Cavalier, over time hostess to all from celebrities to servicemen and guests from all walks of life, has been a true witness to history and a stage for its unfolding. She holds many secrets.

The Mystery Guest
at Tandom's Pine Tree Inn

There are many ways of opening the doors of perception.
Not all of them enable you to control what comes
through the open doors or get them shut again.

~ Guy Lyon Playfair, *The Indefinite Boundary*, 1976

sychics once told a previous owner of the now-gone Tandom's Pine Tree Inn that a "friendly" ghost inhabited the facility (Dougherty, 1990). The inn, opened by the family of J.E. Causey Davis in 1927, was a popular restaurant at 2932 Virginia Beach Boulevard near Lynnhaven Road. Davis ran the restaurant, long known for its fine dining and southern hospitality, the first 50 of its 73 years (Dinsmore, 2001).

Through the years after Davis's ownership, several witnessed the specter and shenanigans of a woman in the restaurant. In 1990, for instance, a woman in the ladies' room saw in the next bathroom stall a pair of feet in button-up, old fashioned style shoes. When she glanced again, the shoed feet had vanished without so much as a sound of someone exiting (Dougherty, 1990). Sometimes the apparition was spotted in the dining area and there was at least one encounter in the kitchen. It seems the specter was especially fond of flipping light switches and draining just-poured drinks.

Oysterman John W. Keeling (1929-2008) was aware of the stories of the inn's ghost, but he thought little of it until the day something happened to him, personally. He arrived one morning, having been hired to shuck oysters for a large event later in the day. Keeling was alone in the kitchen section of the restaurant, immersed in his task in the establishment's "prep" room off the kitchen. Suddenly he heard a large racket from the adjoining kitchen, as if the silverware were being clattered and rattled against one another in the drawer.

Keeling stepped up into the kitchen from where the noise was coming, but there was no one there (Keeling, 2002).

Tandom's Pine Tree Inn closed its doors in July 2000 and was demolished just months afterward. It is said that as the last heap of rubble was pushed aside, the misty shape of a woman rose up from the debris, then settled like dust. Was this perhaps the last appearance of the ghostly woman who had appeared years before?

Pine Tree Inn

Tautog's Restaurant at Winston Cottage

f Tautog's Restaurant does indeed have a ghost, she is a sweet one. This popular beach restaurant with its casual dining style represents a part of Virginia Beach that is rapidly vanishing. It is located in a former beach cottage on 23rd Street that until its present ownership belonged to the builders of the cottage, the Winston family. Built in part in the Arts and Crafts style of the times and having had only two owners since its construction in 1926, the house retains a lot of its original charm and character.

Agnes Winston is believed to be the "ghost" experienced by one of the restaurant's previous staff. Agnes, daughter of surfman Ben Simmons of the nearby Seatack Life-Saving Station (now the Old Coast Guard Station), had grown up on 24th Street very near her future home, Winston Cottage. Before her death at age 93, she was the last living child of a surfman of the old 1878 United States Life-Saving Station. In fact, she had served for many years as a docent at the museum in the "new" (1903) Life-Saving/Coast Guard Station, preserving history by donating some of her father's gear and sharing many true-life stories of his on-the-job exploits.

Agnes outlived her husband and continued to reside in the cottage until 1992, at which time she moved to a retirement home. Anxious about selling her home as she was fearful of its destruction,

Mary Beth, former cook

52

Fact and fiction combine in this sophisticated and intimate form of entertainment. Spiritualism is reborn in an authentic and spine-tingling recreation of a victorian era seance...

→≫≹ The **Seance** ≹≪←

at the

Royal London Wax Museum

1606 Atlantic Ave.

The Séance, yet another attraction in the Bayne Theatre building, was for a period of time upstairs from *The Royal London Wax Museum*. This event was not for everyone: only adults, and even then only the stoutest of heart, were permitted. Participants of the séance sat at a large, round table in a dim parlor with Victorian era furnishings and realistic prompts. The "Medium" led his guests through a mystery, which was eventually solved through the spine-tingling séance procedure. For authenticity, he incorporated personal "readings" which further bewildered his guests. The guide was apparently quite adept at keeping participants "on the edge" of both their psyches and their seats. Even though Johnson and his staff were careful to stress that the séance was staged, so realistic was the feigned experience to a few, that afterward they pulled Johnson or the Medium aside with sincere requests to be put in touch with their dear departed ones (Johnson, 2004).

The attraction's Medium who delivered the frights received one himself one day, shared Johnson. The man was alone and in costume in the parlor, rehearsing his script with his tape recorder on so he could listen to and make refinements to his delivery. An unexplained loud banging on one of the parlor walls stopped him mid-sentence. Johnson, who later heard the audiotape, recalled, "He sits down; there's silence but you can hear him shuffling through his papers. Suddenly you hear the wall banging again... even on the tape it is very loud. Then you hear him gathering his papers and he mumbles something like, 'I'm getting out of here now.' He cuts off the tape recorder and leaves."

For those readers who regret having missed the *Séance*, you may still have a chance to participate. Johnson is considering offering the uncanny attraction at some point in the future. For updates, go to www.youwillscream.com.

Chapter 4

Haunts of Historic Homes & Former Homesites

*I have lost count of the number of times I have spent
a night in 'the most haunted room' of the hundreds
of haunted houses that I have visited, of the thousands
of cases of alleged haunting that have come to my attention;
but still there is a definite excitement in learning
about a fresh haunting, for there is always the possibility
that this venture into the unknown may bring
a never-to-be-forgotten experience, or better still,
that this may be the spontaneous phenomenon
that will prove for all time
the objective reality of such activity.*

~ Peter Underwood, *A Host of Hauntings,* 1973

Adam Thoroughgood House

Whatever else, indeed, a "ghost" may be,
it is probably one of the most complex phenomena in nature.

~ F.W.H. Myers (Quoted in A. Mackenzie,
Hauntings and Apparitions, 1982)

fter the historic Adam Thoroughgood House's last major restoration project began in 1957, occasional reports of strange occurrences started to trickle in. Reported experiences usually occurred in an upstairs bedroom. One such episode involves the witnessing of a depression in the bed that sent tourists and tour guide alike screaming and running down the stairs, a response that lent action to the expression "beat feet."

Many others claim to have witnessed unexplained movements of inanimate objects in the house, such as candlesticks and glass candle domes. Leslie Workman (2003), a previous area resident, recalled a time when the staff would rearrange the furniture only to arrive the next morning and find it exactly the way it was before. Other people alleged seeing a woman, supposedly Adam Thoroughgood's wife Sarah, walking about in the evenings holding a candle in her hand. Regarding this particular claim, at times folks may have been witnessing real-life Margaret Lindemann, then curator of the house, as she and Norrie Martin habitually dressed in 17th century apparel to represent Sarah and Adam Thoroughgood, respectively (McDevitt, 1967). Reports of strange events and sightings dwindled off some time in the 1970s.

The Field Hands of Yesteryear

Odd events at Adam Thoroughgood House dwindled but did not die in the 1970s. More than a decade later, one of the authors attended an afternoon meeting at the old house. Her story is as follows:

It was a May afternoon in 1999. I remember it well. I drove to Parish Road as I was to attend a meeting at the Adam Thoroughgood House. Upon arriving I noticed a vehicle with out-of-state plates in the parking area. As I was approaching the walkway to the house, I realized I had forgotten my notebook. I about-faced and returned to my car to retrieve it. The visitors from the other car stopped me and asked if the house was open to the public. I replied yes, but not at this time; it was now off-hours and I was only there to attend a meeting. The group of four asked questions and because I was early, I was obliged to answer. They told me they had just seen workers in the yard beyond the house, dressed in what looked to be colonial clothes. As the visitors had walked toward them, the workers went behind the building. The visitors thought they could go in for a tour but when they followed the workers, no one was to be seen.

This has not been the only time workers from the past have been seen in this area. If you talk to some of the first residents in the vicinity of Parish Road, they will tell you of strange sightings in the area as it was being developed. Always, workers in the fields have been spotted. They don't stop, they don't look up; they just disappear behind the building. One woman told me that the sun had caught her eyes and when she shaded them with a hand to see more clearly, the costumed people had vanished.

That May afternoon, I questioned the person on duty as I myself wanted to know: was anyone in costume working in the yard within the last hour? The reply I got just added to the stories I had heard before: "No, no one was in the yard working."

The Adam Thoroughgood House in the Bayside area of Virginia Beach is believed by historians to be one of the oldest brick houses in America. More refined dating techniques now cast doubt on earlier assertions that this was the home of early settler and prominent citizen of the area, Adam Thoroughgood (1602 – 1640). That the house was most likely built much later discounts the identity of the afore-mentioned candle-carrying specter as Sarah. However, the house is still thought by historians to have been in the Thoroughgood family.

The Adam Thoroughgood Foundation purchased the house in 1957. The historic home was given to the City of Norfolk by the Foundation on March 21, 1961 (Norfolk Museum Bulletin, 1961). The ownership transferred to the City of Virginia Beach at a "passing of the key" ceremony on October 1, 2003. Among the many people present for the event were the mayors of Virginia Beach and Norfolk and Paul Treanor, a descendant of Adam Thoroughgood (Dunphy, 2003).

The Adam Thoroughgood House, located at 1636 Parish Road, Virginia Beach, Virginia is open for tours. Call for hours of operation and admission fees. The telephone number is: (757) 460-7588.

Carraway Jake

Somewhere in time's own space
There must be some sweet pastured place
Where creeks sing on and tall trees grow
Some paradise where horses go,
For by the love that guides my pen
I know great horses live again.

~ Stanley Harrison

n August of 1968, we moved into an old farmhouse behind the Kempsville fire station. Our son Ronnie, in one of his exploratory modes, one day ventured out into his new surroundings and found an old family cemetery behind an old brick house. A year later, our family moved away.

In April of 1988, our family moved back to Virginia Beach, but to another location. As a lover of history and the realization that our city was packed with its own, I began researching at the local library. I checked out every book I could find for information about Kempsville. In my readings, I found an old map of the town which included its historic Pleasant Hall: I copied the map.

Using the map as my guide, I drove to my previous neighborhood at the corner of Princess Anne and Kempsville Roads. The old house we had lived in years ago was gone: Ronnie's climbing tree behind the barn was all that remained. The fire department had taken up in a new building behind its old one. The former fire station was now a seafood restaurant.

I suddenly realized that the old brick house around the corner from where we had lived was one and the same as the historic Pleasant Hall on the old map. The little house at the edge of the woods was the Carraway House, and the cemetery Ronnie had discovered so many years back was the Carraway family plot. A private business had set up in the Carraway House. I pulled into its parking lot and headed out back, where I did indeed find the cemetery.

I returned to the Carraway cemetery years later for historical information, my tape recorder in hand so as to take oral notes. I walked among the gravestones and recorded each name. Then I spied a headstone standing apart from the others. It was simply marked "Jake." I asked myself aloud, "Who the heck was Jake?" I walked around the tombstones one last time to double-check for accuracy, still wondering who Jake was. I popped into the Carraway House to see if those folks had any information, but they were clueless, even unaware of the cemetery's existence.

When I got home, I carefully transcribed all of the information from my taped notes. At the end of the tape, I heard myself ask, "Who the heck was Jake?" Then I got the shock of my life: a voice responded, "Jake was my horse."

The tombstone marked Jake is now missing, but its base is still there.

~ Deborah Berry

Carraway House

In the small village of Kempe's Landing, a new landowner, James Carraway, acquired some property in 1733 upon which a house was built, today known as the Carraway House. It was not until 1778 when Kempe's Landing became known as a small but bustling commercial port that the county seat was moved there, signifying the largest center of population. In 1783 the village incorporated into the town of Kempsville. The county seat remained in Kemps Landing until 1824 when a county courthouse was built at its current site which represented a more geographically-centered location for all of Princess Anne County.

The Carraway House represents a fine example of a middle class family dwelling of the period. The oldest part of the house is intact as is the addition from the 1800s. The small kitchen "house," originally a separate building, was connected to the house in the twentieth century. Not standing in the way of progress but instead of bulldozing the house, the owners had it moved from its original location and relocated a bit to the northwest when Witchduck Road was first extended in the 1960s. It is remarkable that this little frame dwelling has survived amidst all of the changes that have taken place in Kempsville. It has done so probably because it remained in the Carraway family until 1979 (Mansfield, 1989).

The Ghost of
Woodhouse Manor

*One often hears of a horse that shivers with terror, or of a dog that howls
at something a man's eyes cannot see, and men who live primitive lives
where instinct does the work of reason are fully conscious of many things
that we cannot perceive at all. As life becomes more orderly,
more deliberate, the supernatural world sinks farther away.*

~ W. B. Yeats, Preface to *Lady Gregory's*
Complete Irish Mythology, 1904

ajor Jonathan Woodhouse owned the property on which stands this two-story Dutch gambrel home off today's London Bridge Road. It is surmised that either he or his son William built the house in 1760 as this is the year etched in a brick beside one of the dwelling's doors. The Woodhouse family goes far back in the area's history, from the year 1637 when Captain Henry Woodhouse, an Englishman who had served as governor of Bermuda, claimed a land grant from King Charles I and became one of the area's large landowners in the area south of London Bridge and Oceana.

Several generations of the Woodhouse family lived in the home and on portions of the original land tract before it finally passed out of the family (Princess Anne Hunt Club brochure, undated). William Butt (1897 – 1936) purchased the home in 1913 and farmed the land until his death, which occurred on the premises. The story of his tragic death is set during the tropical hurricane that hit the Atlantic coast on September 18, 1936. While attempting to remove a team of horses from the wind-threatened barn to a safe place, the man was struck on the head by a large, airborne piece of tin that had ripped off the building's roof. The blow knocked him unconscious, in which state his family carried him to the house. He died a few days later from the fatal concussion, to become the lone fatality from the 1936 hurricane (*Virginia Beach News*, 1936). The ghost of Mr. Butt is believed to be the haunt of the Woodhouse home who has made himself known to its occupants from four decades past to the present day.

According to Phyllis M. Capwell, Mr. Butt's shenanigans began in the early 1960s when her mother, Josephine ("Jo") Midgett, purchased about 200 acres of farmland surrounding the old Woodhouse abode (Capwell, 2004). Jo formed a partnership with like-minded individuals who wanted to settle into untainted country living. These people purchased subdivided "farmets," which were at least 10 acres each. The legalese drawn up by Jo's attorney deeded the immediate five acres around the old Woodhouse residence to the organization of landowners.

Initially, the house was left alone in its unwired, unplumbed, and somewhat dilapidated condition. Phyllis recalled those times at dusk when she and her brother would walk across the pasture to the barn to feed the horses. More than once, she claimed, the two would see a light bobbing and moving about in the house. "It seemed someone was searching for something," she said. Neither she nor her brother entered the house at night.

Eventually, the landowners re-formed the Princess Anne Hunt Club, a foxhunting group. The Woodhouse dwelling underwent basic renovation for use as their hunt club. The children, women and men had a merry time with their sport and related festivities, including breakfasts and parties. Mr. Butt, if he was "there," apparently did not mind. Said Phyllis of the house ghost during the hunt club days, "Mr. Butt loved big get-togethers and he was especially happy when his house was full of children." (Unbeknownst to Phyllis, he had fathered nine children of his own!).

It is Phyllis' recollection that Mr. Butt was particularly fond of moving objects about the house and making noises. She avowed, "He was a very mischievous character with a wonderful sense of humor." When Phyllis married in the summer of 1969, she and her new husband initially stayed in what their family referred to as the "Sweet Potato Cottage" on the premises. Abundant in charm and romance, alas, the newlyweds' cottage had no plumbing. Therefore, the two would have to take the short trek to the "big" house for showering and other tasks that required running water. During Phyllis' visits to the house, Mr. Butt would invariably remove things from the sink. These items could usually be located elsewhere in the house, except for the sponges. "He loved my sponges," Phyllis puzzled, amused. "I wouldn't get those back."

While Phyllis feels that Mr. Butt tended to like young women, he seems to have shown some discretion, at least in one case. The hunt club ran a summer camp for a period of time, complete with riding and art lessons. The art teacher hired by Jo Midgett took up temporary residence on the second floor of the clubhouse. Recalled Phyllis, this young lady did not enjoy her summer stint at all, as staying in the old house absolutely spooked her. Her complaints included unidentified noises, the sudden dimming of lights, and windows that opened and closed on their own accord. While others tended to coexist harmoniously with Mr. Butt, the art teacher felt she was not wanted there. When the summer camp was over, she very quickly moved out.

By all accounts, the ghost of Mr. Butt, called "Willie" by later residents, has continued to enjoy harmonious relationships with subsequent inhabitants of his home. Nancy Warren became the house's first post-hunt-club resident in 1981. She refurbished it, named the place Willow Oaks Plantation, and planned to open it as an inn. While the old manor house was never operated as the proposed inn, it remained her home for many years. Nancy's bedroom was the one in which Mr. Butt had died many years before. At night, she often felt a "presence" in that room. One of her dogs, a Great Dane who also slept in the room, likewise acknowledged "it." Tragically, a fire destroyed much of the home, including Nancy's wondrous antique furnishings, just one week before she was to host a holiday party. Although most of her precious belongings and most of the house were lost, Nancy was determined to restore it again.

The house's haunted reputation made it difficult for Nancy to find someone willing to work on the restoration project. One man who agreed to do some work reported feeling blasts of wind coming at him when he was atop his ladder. The odd thing about this was that no wind was blowing. The air around him was otherwise still, offering not even breath enough to rustle one leaf on the nearby trees and bushes. These "willies" so spooked the handyman that he told

Nancy he would only do the work if the house were "purged" of its ghost. The handyman arranged the necessary exorcism to his satisfaction. Nancy Warren later sold the house to the current residents, the Bersons, who have their own ghost stories to tell.

Of course, ghost tales of Mr. Butt conveyed with the property. Pat Berson recalled announcing aloud early on, "Willie, now don't you scare me or I'll have to leave!" Apparently he had no intentions of scaring the family as they reported nothing frightening has occurred to them. This is not to say that nothing has happened. For instance, Pat does admit to being unnerved on her first night in the house when she awakened to hear dogs whimpering as if they were wounded. She and her husband heard the baleful sound several times, and it caused Pat such distress that she even crawled under the house to look for a stranded, trapped animal. It was only after Pat told the former homeowner about the sound that she learned of Nancy's two dogs having perished from smoke inhalation during the horrible fire of years back. She then wondered, as had Nancy, if these sounds might have been the pitiful wails of Nancy's ghost dogs. Thankfully, the sound eventually ceased.

Pat Berson believes she has seen Mr. Butt on occasion. More than once while walking in the yard, she has seen out of the corner of her eye "something like a person dressed in overalls or work clothes. He was at the location of the former barn. We knew that was the old barn location because of the position of the pecan trees" (Berson, 2004).

One quick glance back, and the figure was gone. It was at this barn, of course, that Mr. Butt suffered the fatal blow to his head.

William Thomas Butt Dead from Hurricane Injury; Damage Cited

While such strange events have not instilled fear in the Bersons, their nanny did have a fright from Mr. Butt. Shortly after the Bersons moved into the restored old home, they set up a baby monitor in their young son's room. They did not know then that this had been Mr. Butt's room. The nanny was downstairs and happened to hear over the monitor the baby talking with someone. She went upstairs to check and only the baby was there. It frightened her just a bit but then when it happened again on a different day, she began to be concerned. After hearing the disturbing conversation one too many times, the nanny finally got the "willies" so bad that she quit (Berson, 2004).

The Bersons have gotten used to their unseen resident and over the years have noticed things misplaced or temporarily missing. Laughingly, they ascribe these occurrences to Mr. Butt. They are quite used to living in a haunted house.

Result of Violent Storm; Vast Losses Reported.

VIRGINIA BEACH AREA COUNTS SLIGHT DAMAGE

County Sections Suffer Most; Bridges Washed Away and Roads Inundated.

Princess Anne county and Virginia Beach, surveying the damage which followed in the wake of last Thursday and Friday's hurricane, counted one dead and a vast destruction of property in all sections of the area. Although the storm did less damage to Virginia Beach than resulted from the August, 1933 hurricane, property losses throughout the county are reported at a considerably higher figure.

William Thomas Butt, aged 59, residing on the London Bridge-Nimmo highway, popularly known as the Swamp Road, who died Wednesday afternoon from injuries sustained during the storm, was the county's sole fatality and, indeed, the only death reported in the entire state as a result of the hurricane.

Hit by Flying Tin

Last Friday morning, when the storm threatened to demolish his barn, Mr. Butt left his house to remove a team of horses from the building and lead them to a place of safety. While walking back to his house, a large piece of tin was ripped from the roof of the barn and hurled through the air by the wind, striking Mr. Butt on the head and knocking him to the ground. Picked up by members of his family in an unconscious state, he never did regain complete consciousness, dying, according to the statement of his physician, from a concussion of the brain.

70

Ferry Plantation House: Host to Many Ghosts?

Life is pleasant. Death is peaceful.
It's the transition that's troublesome.

~ Isaac Asimov (1920 - 1992)

erry Plantation House, located in the Bayside area of Virginia Beach, Virginia has become an item of interest in terms of some unusual happenings. Chronicled here are a number of different occurrences that have raised speculation that the old plantation house might contain a spirit or two … or more.

Winter of 1900

Ferry's Little Girl

The date was July 10, 2003; the gathering was the 297th anniversary of the trial of Grace Sherwood, better known as the Witch of Pungo. Many guests were visiting on this anniversary of the well-known historic ducking, which included a trial-by-water reenactment. One guest, Tony, a clergyman, had never set foot on Ferry Plantation. He was unaware that ghost stories had been told of the old estate.

The re-enactors of Grace Sherwood's 1706 trial by water were all gathered in the plantation house, as were docents in costume. As Tony walked into the dining room, he was met by the unexpected. A young girl who looked to be of age six to eight appeared wispfully from nowhere and made her way past him, took a few steps, turned, looked over her shoulder and stared at him. He had a feeling she was looking for someone or something she had lost. With a sad look on her face, she then vanished.

Regarding the appearance of the "Little Girl," whom a psychic proclaimed is "Mary," Tony later explained to a docent of the house, "There is nothing sinister or disturbing about her being there." He described her as follows: "She was wearing a dress, not a gown. She did not appear to be dressed in colonial garb. I could not distinguish the color. Her hair was dark and seemed to be formed in ringlets. The dress might have been an everyday dress... not poor in quality or craftsmanship but neither was it of a rich material or adorned with fancy trappings."

Tony is not the only one to have seen this child from the past. Apparently she has been seen playing about the plantation by many. While the house was in its state of abandonment for twelve years from the mid 1980s, many curiosity-seekers, teenagers and adults alike paid it a visit. One day several inquisitive teens entered the unattended house. These teens, while admittedly seeking adventure, would have rather kept the worlds of the living and the dead separate. No sooner had they made their way inside the boarded-up building than one of them chanced upon a child who ran up the back staircase and vanished. The incident was cause enough for the group to flee from the house and never return. The mother of the teen who had seen the waif-like girl recalled that, when telling the story, her daughter had been white as a ghost.

In another such account gleaned from a newspaper article, the little girl, if the same one, was of a different demeanor, not playfully running about as previously observed. This woman had encountered at Ferry Plantation House the apparition of a "'very young, very sad girl with long hair'" (Ford, 1994).

Who was this child? She seems to make herself appear before many: young and old residents of the area, college students working in the house's library, the aforementioned clergyman and teen, and a group of curiosity-seekers. Psychics have said that she wants her story to be known or that she wants something hidden to be uncovered. Will we ever know what the child is trying to tell or show us?

A Shadow from the Sea

A nighttime inhabitant has been spotted moving about in Ferry Plantation House. "Henry," as a psychic has referred to him, is believed to be a former slave from days long past.

Colonist William Walke long ago lived in a stately brick manor 100 feet north of the current Ferry Plantation House. It has been a known fact from records and family journals that Walke had many sailing ships that brought cargo to Virginia from the West Indies. Among his known cargo were sugar, molasses, rum, and tea. During the Stamp Act, when goods were taxed, the hundreds of coves along the coastline offered perfect hideaways for smugglers who wanted to avoid taxation. Along the Lynnhaven River, some of the coves led to plantations. The river, at two fathoms deep (12 feet), had just enough water for the smaller cargo ships to navigate the waterway.

Tunnels are included in several local tales of seagoing vessels and their secret cargo. While vessels were loading goods in the West Indies, the slave runners often managed to get their "live cargo" aboard. Upon reaching the Virginia Coast, it is believed that the slaves bound for the Princess Anne County farms were hidden in a place few might look for them, under the courthouse in a hidden cell or tunnel-like room. It is supposed that they were kept here until they could discretely be sold.

The courthouse of interest here was adjacent to the Walke Manor house on the site of Ferry Plantation, which sits on an isolated piece of land jutting into the bay. Although it is difficult to believe that a tunnel could have existed in a tidal area with a high water table, evidence suggests this courthouse may have had a tunnel from the shore to what would likely have been a holding cell under the courthouse. There is on the property today an area that could have been this underground cell. For many years now that cell has been filled with rubble from the Walke Manor house, which was destroyed by fire in 1828. Archaeological studies are hoped for to determine what the cell is and whether it has or once had any tunnel-like connector to the water. [The authors wonder if an archaic definition of tunnel, "a shallow conduit or recess" (*Merriam Webster's Collegiate Dictionary*, Tenth edition, 1994), applies to these earlier days and this tidal area.]

Rubble apparently has not stopped Henry, the "shadow from the sea," from extending his stay at Ferry. Several persons have reported seeing the figure of a man walking across a room, passing through the wall and then vanishing. A few visitors to Ferry Plantation have expressed strong feelings about this vague inhabitant. It is believed by one psychic that Henry does not want to leave as he has nowhere to go; he has always lived on the plantation. A psychic has relayed that she believes he, in his former life, was each night shackled on the third floor of the east wing. It is there that he is said to have died on the straw bed that he called his own.

Henry does no harm to anyone or anything. He just moves the occasional object out of his way. Does he cling to the old brick building, only venturing out every so often for a walk to the shore? Is he looking for a way to return to the West Indies? Or is this the spirit of someone the sea has taken? Did he die of starvation or dehydration, possibly from mutiny, on one of the many sailing ships of days long past? These apparitions of the sea are not uncommon. If not Henry, will we ever know the identity of Ferry's nightly shadow from the sea?

The Gliding Lady in White

Ferry Plantation on the Lynnhaven River has a colorful past that spans over hundreds of years, and often crosses over into the spirit world. A glimpse or a whisper can be heard in a fraction of time just to let the believer know that there is a longing for a story to be told. It is believed that the Lady in White has remained on the plantation to tell her tale. Owners and neighbors of the plantation, as well as those visiting the grounds have reported multiple sightings over the past century.

Let us set the scene. The year is 1826. The Walke Manor House has visitors that stay at the plantation from time to time, mostly cousins. Picture in your mind's eye a huge brick Manor House, a racetrack, acres of fruit trees and a bounty of legendary oysters.

The men indulged in gambling, drinking, and card parties that ran into the early hours of morning. The women, on the other hand, enjoyed the beautiful countryside with games on the glorious greens and a sip of sherry or mint julep with their tea.

Tragedy strikes. The Lady in White is found at the bottom of the staircase, her lifeless body never again to enjoy the fresh sea air on her face or to hear the laughter of the children she governed for many years. Psychics have reported that her neck was broken and she died instantly. Some say her heel was caught on the hem of her dress; others blame the children at the top of the stairs for her fatal fall.

It is rumored that in her day, this Lady in White enjoyed the race-track as she is seen even today wandering the fields where the clouds of dust and sounds of pony hooves were embedded for many years. Many have seen her, including multiple guests in attendance at an oyster roast on the old plantation. In more recent years, she was spotted on a bicycle on a dirt path, the wistful layered light remnants of her clothing catching the breeze as she pedaled, as if floating on air.

Carl's Story

A good friend of ours, Carl Martin, left Ferry Plantation House on May 13, 2005 very upset. He had been roasting oysters on the grill for a special event at the house. The three authors, in costume, were greeting guests and giving tours at the house that day. Busy, they missed Carl's quick departure. He could not stop shaking and simply told my daughter, Danielle, that he was sorry but he had to go home because he did not feel well.

What I did not know at the time was that Carl had seen something. What he had witnessed was a lady in white who had quickly appeared then disappeared before him. To make matters even more confusing, when he got in his truck and drove to the brick wall of Cheswick Lane on his way out, there she was again, this time riding on an old-fashioned bicycle of the kind that cannot be mistaken for a modern bike, as one wheel is much larger than the other. It really bothered Carl, as it all seemed so real.

Carl did not tell anyone what he had seen until he returned to Ferry the following week to help install some lights on the second floor. As he seemed very nervous in the house, I asked him what was wrong. When he said it was something that could not leave his thoughts, I suspected that he had seen a vision from the past: I had seen that same look on so many faces over the years. He shared that what had occurred the week before had happened again this very morning.

As he was waiting for us in the parking lot, Carl saw the same woman, wearing Victorian style clothing and again riding a big-wheel bicycle. She had ridden past him and turned to the right on the asphalt roadway. In his vision, the asphalt road was a dirt path.

Carl said he did not want to mention his encounters to us, as he was feeling uncertain and afraid of what he had seen. Further, being in his 70's he feared his sightings might be an indication of medical problems. Carl seemed to feel better after sharing his story. His description of the woman fit that of the "gliding lady" reported by others, but now, for the first time, seen riding on a bicycle.

The former dirt path described by Carl was discovered the next winter. When the grass had died, the old path became visible. The path's route came from the nearby dam, turned at the legendary "hanging tree," and continued on to the former location of the hitching posts at the carriage round under the magnolia tree. If it were not for Carl's experience, I would not have known to go looking for this old dirt carriageway. Ferry's spirits have stories to tell to help us piece together the house's history. All we have to do is listen.

Since this story was written, our good friend Carl passed away. We like to think he will return to meet the Lady in White. Only time will tell.

Belinda Nash

Janet's Story

It was Tuesday evening, May 2nd, 2006, 8:50 to be precise. Darkness had fallen on the Ferry Plantation House. I had just left an evening class held at the house and had walked to my car which was parked on the west side of the parking lot. There before my very eyes a form appeared in the shape of a woman in a long flowing white gown. Her face, visible, had definite features of a woman. I felt as if she wanted me to see her because she looked over the porch of the neighboring house, walked away, then returned to the edge of the porch, turned, and walked away again. I noted that she seemed to be gliding rather than walking. She stared into the darkness, seemingly searching for something. Our eyes did not make contact. Goose bumps rose on my flesh as I continued to watch this spirit, who finally turned slowly and vanished into the darkness. In repeating my experience to others, I was relieved to learn that this woman has been sighted over twelve times in the past: I am not alone in experiencing the presence of this gliding lady in white.

Janet L. Wagner

More Encounters

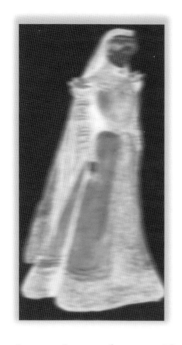

In addition to Carl and Janet, other witnesses have reported a slender, longhaired specter wearing a floor-length gown. At a neighborhood civic league meeting in the 1990s, several stories of the mystery woman surfaced (Ford, 1994). One woman who had spent some time in the house reported being busy in the kitchen when the female figure entered from the dining room, passed her, and disappeared through the pantry door. The two did not make eye contact.

Neighbors of Ferry whose back deck faces the old house had seen what seems to be the same ghostly young woman walk out of their own home's closet and across the room. These neighbors had repeated occurrences of waking up to find their outside chairs moved from the home's deck and placed on the lawn, arranged in a line pointed towards the plantation house. The family has since moved.

When Ferry Plantation House was up for sale in the 1990s, a prospective buyer's daughter, age nine at the time, told her mother, "There's a lady in my room." Although the mystery woman did not speak to her, the child felt certain the two were to share her future bedroom if her family were to purchase the house. No one was found when the parent went looking for the visitor.

While serving as caretaker of the house for five years, Patrick McAtamney had his own brief encounter with the gliding lady. Patrick, his wife, and his daughter Mederise were Ferry's last residents, tenants in the 1980s when the house sat amidst 30 acres of cultivated fields. It was a cold day on the old farm when Patrick witnessed the mysterious lady.

I was in the den enjoying the fire when I saw a transparent figure of a woman come from behind me. My peripheral vision first caught her. Then she came around and all I saw was her back as she came into the downstairs room, the 1850 addition to the house. It was real fast; a quick movement and she didn't turn around, look back or anything. Nothing precipitated her movement like cold air that you hear about. It was already a cold day, but nothing put me on edge or anything. It was so fast. She just came by with no sound. She was wearing a long, flowing one-piece kind of dress, kind of flow-y. What was also weird was her color. She was whitish, transparent looking. It caught me totally off guard and I'd say I didn't detect any steps, like someone walking. It was more like she kind of wisped on by (McAtamney, 2004).

Sally Rebecca Walke

In 1997 a psychic visited Ferry Plantation House. Going from room to room, he told of what he interpreted as paranormal activities "received" through his body. He described each room and its contents from an earlier time. As he made his way from floor to floor, he heard voices. One was of "Sally," whom he said had lost her fiancé in the Civil War. The medium told of a tall dark-haired girl leaning against a mantel.

Interestingly, when the late Calvert Walke Tazewell, Jr. researched the family history, he wrote that Sally Rebecca Walke had lived at the Ferry Plantation House during the Civil War years. The remaining sketch of the woman's life has been gleaned from members of the family who have preserved the past in journals, letters and genealogy.

Sally was born on March 27, 1842. While in her teens she met, fell in love with and became engaged to a young man who entered the Civil War. To this day only his first name, John, is known. As most young ladies did in time of war, she went to live with extended family (in her case, her cousins) while the men and boys went off to fight. It was April 6, 1863 that the news came to Ferry Plantation House, then owned by the McIntoshes, that Sally's young beau would not return.

To her beloved soldier's memory, heartbroken Sally planted a magnolia tree in her cousins' yard at Ferry. It was planted outside the land-side door to grow to the mighty strength and height that it boasts today. It is also said that Sally kept a shrine in remembrance of her lost love on the mantel of the second floor west wing bedroom. On the mantel were lit candles and a snippet of his hair in a locket; his sword hung on the wall above. She truly mourned the loss of her fiancé. Sally passed away on September 18, 1917 at the age of seventy-five, by all indications a spinster (Tazewell, 1991). It has been said that she died of a broken heart.

Although the 1850 mantel over the fireplace has since been replaced, it is assumed that Sally still visits the room she stayed in at Ferry. An occasional visitor who has come to the room has been witness to a tall dark-haired girl leaning against the mantel, sobbing and heartbroken. The faint glow of candles has been seen time after time, accompanied by a smell in the air of fresh-mowed hay. It may be that Sally has come back to wait for her true love to return. It is believed that she does not want to leave this plantation house with its memory of her lost love.

As the years passed the magnolia grew, but its mighty roots pulled it off center of the doorway that it was to shade. But Mother Nature has looked out for Sally and the magnolia tree, for if you look at the tree today you will see how it was pulled aside at the root base and, by some unknown force, now has a curve in its massive trunk that again aligns it with the land-side door. Sally's magnolia tree is today quite large and has been entered in the register of Champion Trees of Virginia. The tree is truly a treasure from the past, compliments of Sally, whose story shall live on.

Sally and the Red Hat Ladies

On Saturday, July 31, 2004, Ferry Plantation House hosted a fashion show for the local Red Hat Society. In the heat of the day and with so many being in the house, it was hard to keep things cool. The models were changing clothes in Sally's room while others, rapidly cooling themselves with fans, were listening raptly as docent Belinda Nash told Sally's story. All of a sudden a cold chill passed through the room. Everyone felt it. Belinda Nash, wearing the full regalia (six layers) of antibellum costume, got goose bumps on her arms and a chill up her spine. She explained to the twenty-some women, "As it was told to me, if you are speaking about a departed one who is present in the room, that departed one will let you know of its presence." It may be that just the suggestion of the story triggered off a surge in all of their bodies, but it is a fact that each and every one of those ladies experienced the collective chill.

Sally's Room

In past years on Halloween nights, the authors would dress in ante-bellum costumes and, along with other volunteers, each "man" a room in Ferry Plantation House to tell its ghost story to the evening's guests. I always offered to take Sally's room, as her story is especially dear to my heart. I would position myself at the fireplace where Sally is typically sighted and tell passers-through about sad Sally's history and quiet haunting.

It was rather late one Halloween night, and the guests had dwindled. Two young ladies who had earlier heard me tell Sally's story had returned upstairs to visit the room and take pictures with their cell phone cameras. The three of us were the only ones in the room. One of the girls suddenly and urgently called me over to her in a loud whisper: "Come here and look at this!" she said. She was pointing the phone to the fireplace where, with the two young ladies I witnessed on the screen a transparent blue, shifting mass. We could not see it through our eyes.

It has been speculated that a spirit will transform to a vaporous state before appearing as a full-bodied apparition. Is that what Sally was doing? Was she trying to show herself to us select few ladies who carried forth and appreciated her story?

~ Deni Norred

Visit at Halloween

To visit the Ferry Plantation house at Halloween or another time of the year, call first, 757-473-5182, to be sure tours are available.

The Case of the Dismanteled Dessert

Another curious story emerged as one psychic toured Ferry Plantation House. He claims to have heard the name, "Eric." This is the name a docent at the old house ascribes to a figure of a small boy who has been seen by several people who have visited the house. By the described size, Eric is a child of perhaps six or seven. Docent Belinda Nash tells the following story to illustrate what a prankster the young man is:

> Two of us volunteers at the house can relate what happened first hand The year was 1997. There were no furnishings in the house and portions of it were still boarded up. It was a cold day with no windows open and heat had not yet been installed in the house. We had a group of students from a local college doing some design work in the house. Three students were in the library with me. Having nowhere to put their things, the students had placed their lunches on the fireplace mantel. One had put a Snickers bar on the end of the mantel.
>
> To set the stage for what was about to happen, please know that we were all in different areas of the room. I was in the doorway facing the mantel with one student beside me. Another student was to the right of the mantel, kneeling and loading her camera. The third was near the parlor door to the left of the fireplace. The room was silent when, all of a sudden, the Snickers bar flew off the mantel. It just looked like someone had whisked it off and it went sailing. We all stared as it hit the floor with a soft thud.
>
> We looked at each other in disbelief and concluded that we were all too far away from it to have touched it. We had heard other stories about objects moving in the house and we wanted to put a clear view on what had just happened. One of us then placed the candy bar on the mantel where it had been originally. Perhaps it had been leaning on something and some little vibration had made it fall. Testing this theory, we could not make it happen,

but with a little push it fell straight to the floor: it didn't fly four feet away as it had done earlier. The other group of students was called into the room to see if they could help us duplicate the happening. It could not be done.

It's been suggested that maybe we had an opossum in the house and we have found traces of an animals leavings, but I'll tell you... it was no opossum that made that candy bar move. I am witness to that.

Was this the mischievous Eric who was playing with the observers' minds as well as sending shivers up their spines? Later, someone suggested putting a ball in the house for Eric to play with. This was done and it often has been found moved from room to room within the Ferry Plantation House.

From the Mouths of Babes

Co-author Belinda Nash, who spends much of her time at Ferry, has been dazzled by her own granddaughter's experiences there. These have been shared in tidbits by the child through her forthright assertions over a number of years.

This story begins when my granddaughter was age two, just learning to talk. Day after day she would come to Ferry Plantation with me, and we would work on all three floors of the house almost all day long. One day in the fall of the year, I shivered. There was an overcast sky. The wind had come up and rattled the shutters as it had done many times before.

I could feel the persistent draft that penetrated between the floorboards and I felt we should work on the second floor that day, as it would be warmer. Making our way to the stairway in the central hallway, little Kathlene climbed to the third stair at the turn and stopped. I was right behind her. She held up her little hand and pointed to the top of the stairs. I could still feel the chill from the draft and it gave me a shiver. She said there was someone up there. I replied to her, "No one is there, it may be the

shadow from the trees," as they were swaying in the breeze. Again she said, "Nanny, someone is there." I picked her up and walked up the stairs to show her that we were alone, even though I had the feeling that we were not. I had not witnessed any paranormal activities in the house before, but have heard footsteps. When I feel something strange, I tend to sing a lot. And so I did.

easily or make a loud noise if damaged. After Papa's death Caitlin asked if she could have a balloon at every birthday as well as Easter and Christmas. She said she wanted to send balloons up to Papa in heaven. Some time later Caitlin's father was at a gathering where there was a psychic. Being a non-believer of the psychic's talents, he nonetheless asked, "Can you tell me about my daughter?" The psychic said an older man visits with her, and this older man says to tell her that he gets the balloons that she sends him.

When Caitlin's Uncle Scott was in a Jet Ski accident and was so badly hurt that he was on life support, Caitlin had said to her grandmother, "Papa says to tell you, Scott will be okay." Many surgeries later, Scott indeed recovered.

Caitlin, at the time of the first publication of this book, was nine years old. She remembers with great fondness the remarkable gentleman who was her teacher and protector, her wonderful Papa who kept his promise to always be there.

Author's Note: While Caitlin and the family live on the original Ferry Plantation land, the memory of Papa lives on as well. Do the spirits want to live on at these grounds? Ferry is a wonderful piece of history that would not have been saved if it were not for the residents of the old plantation going out on a limb to save the historic treasure. Thank you Joe, I know you are still here, as you have helped us in many ways when you were alive and you have continued to help restore the Ferry Plantation House over the years. For the benefit of the reader, please know that it was Joe's $3500.00 that paid for half of the walkway placed in May 2004. To memorialize the families represented by Papa Joe, a granite marker was set in the walkway with the two families' names on it. He does live on at Ferry Plantation.

~ *Belinda Nash*

Little Leather Document Box

Whenever you have eliminated the impossible, whatever remains, however improbable, must be the truth.

~ Arthur Conan Doyle

On the mantel in the library of Ferry Plantation House sits a little leather document box. To some it would have no meaning at all, while to others who have witnessed the attempts that this little box has made to share its message from its past, it has incredible meaning.

At the Annual Strawberry Shortcake Open House in 2001 the Ferry Plantation House was delighted to have this treasure donated by Louise N., a member of the Walke family. Louise had sent down many pictures of the family members so that faces  could be matched to the history of the Plantation. On the bottom of the box was carved in the wood, "This belonged to my grandmother," followed by the owner's name. But who was her grandmother?

Louise had also sent photographs of both sides of the family as the mystery box owner had to be one of the grandparents. The pictures were left in the leather box untouched. Time went by and another relative of the Walke family donated a journal that had been passed down from several generations. While sitting in the library reading parts of this journal, one of the authors (of this ghost book) found the description of this little box: a leather covered document box with brass hobnails down the sides and corners, lined with newsprint.

The box described in the journal was from the Walke Manor House that was on the property prior to the circa 1830 plantation house that stands today. The Walke family grew tobacco among other things. Not knowing of crop rotation and upon depleting the land of its nutrients, this farming family, like others, moved to a new location. They had left for Ohio, allowing family members to use the Walke Manor House as a summerhouse. The little box, apparently belonging to the manor house up to this point, moved to Ohio with the family.

Around 1828 the Walke Manor house burned to the ground leaving nothing but a pile of bricks. In about 1830 the Ferry Plantation House that stands today was built to half the size of the manor house using those good handmade bricks that were unharmed by the manor's fire. More than 150 years has passed and this little leather trunk has found its way back to its original plantation home site to become a part of her history. It is currently the only item on the premises from the former 1751 house.

Now, let's get back to the owner of the little leather "trunk," as it was called on the inscription on the bottom of the box. This was still a mystery, although pieces of the history are slowly unraveling. One July evening a few years later, two members from the Edgar Cayce Foundation came out for a visit. They walked from room to room. They heard names, the same names spoken of many times before. One of the ladies said that she felt something, a very strong sensation, while near the leather box. She wondered if the name Mary-Margaret meant anything to the house. Not as one person's name, a well-informed docent  replied. The woman from the foundation asserted that Mary-Margaret had been the owner of the box. Among the pictures that had been given to Ferry by Louise was one of Elizabeth in the lap of her mother, Mary and one of Elizabeth's grandmother Margaret.

Could it be that the grandmother passed the leather box to the grandchild and then to Louise, who gave it to Ferry? Stranger things have happened. Items of history have a peculiar way of traveling back home.

93

Margaret, Mary and Elizabeth have been roaming in the library and have been seen since 2001: you can even feel the ladies as they near you. Many of Ferry's visitors on day tours say that they can feel the energy from the leather box. You yourself can stand near it and talk to a stranger about it and goose bumps will likely rise on your flesh, and a chill run up your spine. Some say that this is a sign of a truth wanting to be told.

This little leather-covered box with the brass hobnails is very dear to the docents at Ferry. Ferry Plantation House has had its share of strange events and this one is not finished yet. The leather box may be trying to tell something. When the time and circumstances are right, no doubt the whole story of the Little Leather Document Box will be revealed.

Stella and the Wild Mushrooms

All mushrooms are edible – once.

~ Anonymous source

Charles Mitchell Barnett and his wife Stella Crowder Barnett moved to Norfolk in the late 1800s and built a handsome brick home that still stands on Fairfax Avenue. Their daughter Jean was born before this time, in Mexico City, and two boys, Charles Jr. and Joseph were soon added to the family (Brown, 2004).

In 1896 the Barnetts purchased Old Donation Farm, following a dream of Charles' to enjoy country living and farming. His success in business was with the railroad companies, which led to worldwide travel and expanding interests in coal and shipping. Eventually, the time came to settle with the family and enjoy the farm in Princess Anne County. Major crops grown on the extensive acreage of Old Donation Farm included strawberries, cabbage, wheat and spinach. In the bay just beyond the house, the famous Lynnhaven Bay oyster clusters were plentiful. These were harvested and shipped to many places, including the Waldorf Astoria Hotel and the famous Grand Central Station Oyster Bar in New York City (Brown, 2004).

In 1912 the family sustained a shocking loss when Stella became ill after eating wild mushrooms that she had picked in the field beyond their home. Son Charles, then a boy of twelve, was sent on horseback to fetch the doctor. When he arrived, the doctor found that Stella had made her way up the steep stairway to the second floor, to the room now referred to as the Green Room in Ferry Plantation House. It was there that Stella fell into a coma from the poison in a mushroom that fooled even these usually expert gatherers. She died three days later.

Charles Sr. had, in those years, been traveling extensively in South America and Africa in his capacity as a respected expert in the shipping and mining industries. Soon after Stella's death, he sent for her sister, Cora

Crowder, to come and help look after the children and the household. It took Cora several months to return by ship, as she was then serving as a missionary/nurse in the Middle East. She comforted the bereft family and eventually became the second Mrs. Barnett (Brown, 2004).

Today there is a picture of Stella and Cora in the Green Room of Ferry Plantation House. It has been reported on several occasions that someone of Stella's description has been seen in the Green Room going about her duties. It was not until July of 2003 that the identity of the Green Room visitor was discovered. Putting all the family history, stories and sightings together, a description was formed that matched that of Stella.

One person said he had heard a muffled sound, as if someone were choking. He thought that possibly the sound was coming from downstairs. But no, this sound could not carry up the stairwell. This person was not aware of other sounds that have been heard in the house. On another occasion, from the same room, there was a constant moaning heard. Could this be the sound of someone in pain from eating poisonous mushrooms? Did Stella leave with unfinished business to complete? Is that why she remains at the house? Perhaps she has wanted to keep a watchful eye over her family and her beloved home.

The presence of Stella does not alarm anyone. Those who visit the house for tours, having no idea of her history, say that as they enter, a feeling of warmth and belonging overcomes them. Ever the hostess, Stella was responsible for many happy gatherings on the plantation. The annual oyster roasts were held at the "ferry landing," and Ferry Plantation House has a collection of many photos of these and of July 4th gatherings up until 1912.

Today in the spring and in wet summer weather one can see many mushrooms of all varieties growing on the original plantation. No one knows for sure if the predecessors of these are what caused Stella's death. Family members passed down the information to the present generation. Knowing this story makes one think before taking this delicious treat to the dinner table. Maybe Stella wanted this story told, to warn others about harvesting and eating the wrong wild mushrooms.

Continued History of Old Donation Farm

Several years after Cora Barnett moved to the Old Donation Farm, she took over the entertaining. There are many old newspaper clippings that tell of some events during the early 1920s and into the 40s. One article reported, "Over a thousand persons came to see the play 'Two-Mile Tree' that was performed on the land-side porch. Guests enjoyed lemonade and ice-cream at the May Festival" (*Virginian-Pilot* & the *Norfolk Landmark*, 1931). The Women's Club of Princess Anne County hosted the festivals. Every May, a historic site was the topic of a play written by Mary Sinton Leitch (1876-1954). Three of these plays were enacted at Old Donation Farm (Brown, 2004).

Charles Barnett Sr. continued to own and operate the Old Donation Farm even after he and Cora moved to New York City. They returned as often as possible to visit. Close friend and joint owner Jim Hudgins conducted the farm business. Charles Sr. died in 1940, of a heart attack that occurred at the Waldorf Astoria Hotel in New York City, where he often went and enjoyed the famous Lynnhaven Bay oysters still shipped to the Waldorf from the bay beyond his own farm (Brown, 2004).

Charles Mitchell Barnett Junior, who continued to run the farm for many years with Mr. Hudgins as a managing partner, inherited Old Donation Farm after his father's death. Every year from 1945 until 1949, a case of strawberries was sent to Catherine (Bunny) Barnett Brown, at Sweet Briar College near Amherst, VA. Arrival of this home farm fruit was always an occasion for a dormitory ice cream and berries party (Brown, 2004).

A Quiet Meeting on the Stairs

To set the scene for you, it was September and the August Children's History Camps had ended. A lot of clothing had been laundered with so many children having attended the last two weeks of camp. In addition to the children, our junior and adult docents who had helped with the camps had all been wearing costumes of the 1700s and 1800s. These many layers of linen, all washed and ironed, were ready to be stored on the third floor in the costume closet at the Ferry Plantation House.

I (Belinda Nash) had already made two trips up to the third floor. Visitors to the house that day had just finished their tour and were now in the second floor hallway above the stairs, waiting to get into the gift shop. I was not in costume this day, just wearing a sweater and jeans, again making my way up the first flight of stairs carrying two armloads of clothing. When I had reached the halfway point, I felt a nudge. I lost my balance and dropped the clothing from my right hand to grab the handrail to steady myself. Our visitors at the top of the stairs looked down at the bit of commotion that had occurred. One woman looking at me said, astonished, "There is a handprint on your sweater." I looked down at my chest and I too could see the print that was left in the jersey material, only to see it fade away. Another onlooker asked, "What made this happen?" I thought for a second and replied, "We do have a few visitors in the house that we now and again come in contact with but they are all friendly."

My own comment prompted me to think for awhile as I picked up the clothing and continued to the next set of stairs to the third floor. At no set times in the house, day or night, were the staircases ever known to be "busy" with spirits. Sometimes it is thought that children are playing on the stairs as visitors have heard hollow laughter with a slight echo to it. I wondered again about the nudge that I had felt and the handprint that had disappeared.

I asked myself, was this presence trying to push me? If so, why? As far as I know, we have never had any unwanted or angry spirits wandering around in the house since I have been here and this was now my fourteenth year. We even had the house blessed by a priest in 2002. I felt that I must look at this situation again. Now sitting in the Nanny's third floor room, a very peaceful room that clears one's mind, I gave this quite a bit of thought. Each time I enter the house, as I walk in I place my hands on each side of the door casing and silently ask permission to enter, assuring whomever may be *listening that I will do nothing to remove any presence from this dwelling. I do believe that we have a few "caretakers" still looking after this old manor house. I refer to them as "soul prints" that have been left behind so that their individual stories can be told. These spirits of the past may have stayed on for over 180 years. This historic house could never scare me away. In fact, it is actually sometimes a comfort to believe that I am not alone in the house.*

Thinking all of this over, I concluded that nothing that abides within Ferry Plantation House would try to harm me here. I strongly believe that the presence I felt on the stairway was trying to slow me down, as I do have high blood pressure and sometimes tend to rush. Maybe I was being protected from a potential fall?

You may have heard the old saying, "If walls could talk..." I hope our walls never stop talking.

~Belinda Nash

A Veil of Fog Over Ferry

The fog is like a cage without a key.

~Elizabeth Wurtzel

The day was bright and sunny, very warm. Dr. Nathanial Stolow, assessor from The Conservation Assessment Program, was doing a three day research project on the Ferry Plantation House to approve a grant having to do with artifact exhibitions. He had had endless trouble with his equipment not working in the house: batteries constantly going dead; chargers not keeping their charge. Three of Dr. Stolow's cameras had stopped working and, although our video camera appeared to be working, on playback it had filmed nothing. More pictures had to be taken outside as the assessor had none to show in his $7,000.00 report.

I went out to my car to fetch my own camera. I took pictures on the land side of the house for more than fifteen minutes while Dr. Stolow showed me the angles that he wanted. We then went around to the river side where who should appear walking up the brick path but Al Chewning, author of *Haunted Virginia Beach*. He stopped to see what we were doing.

Al asked, "Belinda, any new ghost stories to tell?" I introduced him to Dr. Stolow. Knowing that we had to get on with the photo shoot for the report, Al then asked if he could pick up some more ghost books as he was going to need them to sell at an event. I sent him into the house, as Al knew where to find them. I remained outside and waited while Al entered the house. The door shut and then the strangest thing happened. As I raised the camera to take a picture, it seemed like the lighting outside turned dimmer with Mother Nature at the control board. Both Dr. Stolow and I commented on the change. I cannot explain why but it gave us an eerie feeling and made us want to go inside.

It wasn't until I went to print these pictures off for Dr. Stolow's report that we noticed this one photograph showing a haze or fog around the house. It wasn't just our eyes that had noticed a dramatic shift in the atmosphere, the camera had caught it as well. The pictures taken before Al had asked about ghost stories turned out just fine.

Very coincidental, I must say. The camera had been with me during the last nine pictures. It had been a sunny afternoon with no humidity and no temperature change. No storm had been approaching and it was many hours before nightfall. And yet this picture appeared, with the look of the morning mist as I recalled from a trip... a strange dense fog rising up from a heathered moor in Scotland. The foggy look at Ferry created a veil between the house and sky. Very odd, indeed.

~ Belinda Nash

The Cloudy Side of Sunnyside

And round about his home, the glory
That blushed and bloomed
Is but a dim-remembered story
Of the old time entombed.

~ Edgar Allan Poe, *The Haunted Palace*

t was 1963 when Page Herbert came upon a chance to purchase the lovely Sunnyside, a plantation house built around 1833 and set on a sprawling land tract belonging to distant relatives. He jumped on the opportunity and eagerly acquired the real estate. Just before Page and his family were to move in, the former owner, Aunt Lottie, moved out, but not in the usual sense. Unfortunately, perhaps, for the new residents, Lottie died in the house.

As was the custom, friends and relatives prepared Lottie's body for viewing. Being in the house alone with the body before the internment did not appeal to Bessie, Lottie's housekeeper, but stay she did. Reportedly, she was terrified.

Lottie was properly buried and very soon the property was occupied by the new Herberts. The housekeeper and gardener were kept on as employees. Bessie began to believe very strongly that Aunt Lottie had not moved on "to the next world" and was, in fact, "residing" in a part of the house that was seldom used: the attic.

At a nearby point lived Mildred (a fictional name), a relative of the Herberts whose father had at one time resided at Sunnyside. Mildred once told Page Herbert a chilling story about the house. One day Mildred the child was playing in the attic and the room suddenly filled with fog. She saw a figure in the fog, panicked, and fled. The figure was not clearly identifiable, but one can only guess what tales the housekeeper and the neighbors shared. Even in her adult years, Mildred occasionally claimed seeing lights in Sunnyside's attic window.

For 27 years, Page Herbert and his family lived in the house that had been in the family since it was built. In spite of their agreement that the house was not haunted in the typical Hollywood tradition presented in scary movies, the Herberts concur that the house definitely "had something going on" (Herbert, Elizabeth, 2003). Nonetheless, they harbor mostly fond memories of the place. This is not to say that strange occurrences did not happen: they did. For example, when Mrs. Herbert would aesthetically arrange her what-nots on the marble fireplace mantel, the items were invariably rearranged the next morning. The unidentified phantom culprit, seemingly offended by candlesticks set at opposite ends of the mantel, habitually placed them together at one end!

The son, also named Page in his family's tradition, is uncertain if some of the stories were actually attached to his childhood home or were merely universal "old house" tales begged, borrowed, and embellished in one's youth. Family lore included one tale of a distant uncle who, during the Civil War, packed all the family silver in a trunk and buried it on the property to save it from Union hands. This story's theme is one shared by many Southerners and probably in many instances is true: what better hiding place could there be for family valuables? Page and his sister Elizabeth grew up scouring the premises for what in their memory was the legendary "pair of silver pistols." Supposedly, the stash remains buried on the grounds of Sunnyside to this day.

Another odd and interesting story emerges. Young Page Herbert, while a student at Kempsville High School, once hosted a party in the driveway of his family's home. A friend accompanied by his new girlfriend made an appearance. The girl was introduced around and the two stayed a short while, then left. A few weeks later, Page ran into the girl again. She relayed a wild dream she'd had about the Herbert's house, which she had never entered. In the dream, the girl knocked on the door and entered. She was facing the stairway and hallway. Her description to Page was a match to the house's entryway. She entered a room to the right (there was one in the Herbert house), obtained a lit candle, and proceeded up the stairs, candle in hand.

The girl's nightmare, as she told it to Page, continued to correctly describe the layout of the rooms upstairs. She turned toward one bedroom doorway, where she encountered her boyfriend ... with half his face missing.

Erie enough, but just a dream, right? Page shared the girl's grisly nightmare with his father. In turn, Mr. Herbert informed his son that, in the very bedroom in which the girl dreamt the encounter with her disfigured boyfriend, a man had many years ago committed suicide by shooting himself in the face.

Whether or not this really happened (Mr. Herbert is actually unaware of any tragedies having occurred in the house), the anecdote certainly made for a good story to frighten young Page. Further, one could say that the girl's dream at least hints of spatial precognition as she could mentally map the design of Sunnyside's rooms even though she had never entered the house.

So what is Sunnyside's story? Last owner in residence Page Herbert shared that Edward Henry Herbert (1806-1862) gave the plantation, originally impressive in its acreage, to his daughter Laura and her husband, Dr. James N. McAlpine as their wedding present. In its day, Edward Herbert's own expansive farm on the other side of Indian River turnpike, "Level Green," was said to be "one of the best conducted farms" in the county (Yarsinske, 2002). For the newlyweds, he had the magnificent gift of Sunnyside built in the Kempsville area, on the Elizabeth River.

The McAlpines were Sunnyside's first residents. One of the house's wings supposedly served as the Dr. McAlpine's office. During the Civil War, the doctor was appointed staff surgeon in Brigadier General Armistead's Brigade (Tagg, 1998). Colonel E. C. Edmonds of his regiment lauded McAlpine for "the faithful manner" in his "bearing off the wounded amid the leaden hail." Of the surgeon and his assistant, the Colonel further boasted, "The one snatched them from the mouth of the cannon, the other from the jaws of death" (United States War Department, et al., 1884). As true of all surgeons' work during the Civil War, McAlpine's was certainly a grisly duty; his house aside, surely the amputations, mutilations, and loathsome deaths haunted the man himself!

Said descendant Dave Herbert of hauntings at the house, "My

Aunt told me that one time when she stayed at Sunnyside she swore she saw a ghost coming up the stairs. She said it was a woman dressed in a long flowing white dress" (Herbert, 2003). As this sighting would have predated Lottie's death, one might wonder if the ascending ghost was Laura in her wedding gown. Alternatively, perhaps it was Laura in her nightdress, returning to bed after assisting her husband as he tended to a late-night medical emergency in his downstairs office. It could be argued that either Laura or Lottie would later rearrange the fireplace mantel's knickknacks to her liking.

Laura Herbert McAlpine lived past the age of ninety. She was said to have melodiously charmed others with "her delightful little songs," even in her latter years (Kellam & Kellam, 1958). After she passed away, the Sunnyside manor went on to offer its walls and warmth to Herbert relations for many years. It was, in its last decades until 1987, the home of Page Herbert, his wife, and their children. Sadly, Sunnyside was demolished in 1990. Thanks to the Herberts, however, its legacy lives on … and, really, it is mostly a sunny legacy.

Strange Occurrences at Upper Wolfsnare Plantation

Tough tellin' not knowin'.

~ Old Vermont saying

n the day they moved into the historic home, the young couple who agreed to be the caretakers of Upper Wolfsnare Plantation had no cause for worry. The story they communicated several years later begins as a tale of any moving day, anywhere, with the exception of one strange twist. After several trips by car, they finally had all of their belongings in the old house.

Andy and Hannah (not their real names) had agreed that since part of the historic house was open to the public, they would leave these several rooms untouched and put all of their things in the basement. "This is one of the very few homes in Virginia Beach that has a real basement," Hannah said. Since the basement was cleared out long ago, this was the one room in the house in which they could put all of their boxes with room to spare. It was the perfect place to organize the possessions that would be moved to the second floor, their personal part of the house. Everything was going perfectly until Andy stopped moving items from boxes and suddenly stood absolutely still.

Someone was moving, walking directly over the floorboards above him. He watched as the boards overhead reverberated with each step. He thought Hannah was on the second, not the first floor. The realization that someone else might be in the house spurred him to action. Quickly, he flew up the stairs to the first floor to find…no one. He called, "Where are you?" Hannah answered from upstairs. He called, "Were you just down here?" Her answer was, "No."

"OK," he thought, "weird." He looked all around on the first floor, checking all of the rooms, even looking outside. Seeing nothing unusual but taking no chances, he locked all of the doors to the outside. He went back down into the dusky basement. Ripping tape from a box, he heard something now unnervingly familiar. The footfalls on the floor directly above again startled him. Spying a baseball bat, he grabbed it on the run and bounded as fast as he could up the stairs. No one was there. "Hey!" "What?" Hannah upstairs responded; "What's wrong?" "You won't believe this," and he commenced to tell her what had just happened.

After this incident, no more footfalls were heard, but other sounds would often awaken the two or cause them to lose sleep. "The best way to describe it is like someone was whispering. We never could hear distinct words, but it was like 'they' were just in the next room. It was creepy, and we never got used to it. I never did feel really comfortable there alone," admitted Hannah. These sounds never ceased during the couple's stay in the house and for the several years that the two lived there, they felt as if they were sharing the residence with an unknown entity. They never felt threatened, just a little uneasy.

But theirs was not the only unusual experience a resident of the historic Upper Wolfsnare Plantation has reported. On several occasions, a daughter of former curators of the home had seen the lurking figure of a scowling man wearing clothing of a bygone era. Penelope Taylor reported seeing the man once in her bedroom in 1980 and again in the living room three years later. She had fled terrified, in the first instance, and closed her eyes tightly and pretended sleep in the second. She believed the spirit to be that of Thomas Walke IV, the son of the house's builder, who died in his early thirties (Giametta, 1984). Members of the Princess Anne/Virginia Beach Historical Society who manage the house have not been able to verify or confirm these stories. They do say that the clothing described by Penelope is not of the period related to Thomas Walke IV.

The Upper Wolfsnare Plantation manor, built around 1759 by Thomas Walke III, is near Wolf Snare Point. The place was also known as Brick House Farm. Our purported ghost, son Thomas IV, was one of the two local representatives to the Virginia Convention of 1788, which decided Virginia would ratify the recently drafted Constitution of the United States.

Upper Wolfsnare Plantation

Located at 2040 Potter's Road, this brick Georgian home is open noon to 4 p.m. Wednesdays, July through August or by group appointment. Call the Princess Anne County/Virginia Beach Historical Society, the current owners, at (757) 473-5182.

The Ghost of
Longview House

If we could take a material man and dissolve away his physical constituent without interfering with the sense-data by means of which we perceive him, we should be left with, exactly, an apparition.

~ G.N.M. Tyrrell, *Apparitions*, 1953

he old brick Longview/Whitehurst/Buffington house near the Virginia Beach Municipal Center is now owned by the City of Virginia Beach. Its previous owners, Jay and Emily Buffington, heard from county residents that the house was haunted even before they bought it in 1953. While skeptical at first, their very first night in the house converted them to believers. From their upstairs bedroom, the couple heard the dogs "having a fit" on the floor below. Jay was, in his daughter Ann's words, "too yellow" to go downstairs and check out the source of the ruckus. In the morning, the Buffingtons intrepidly crept downstairs and found all their furniture rearranged (Buffington, 2004).

This first-night initiation did not frighten off the Buffington family. They acknowledged the house was haunted and in spite of other mysterious high jinks that occurred, they were not afraid. Mrs. Buffington once recounted a bell-pull in the dining room flying across the room. Another time, all the dining room lights turned off simultaneously, even though on different circuits. Doorknobs would turn; water spigots would turn on and off.

It was local belief that the house's ghost was that of James Howard Whitehurst (1843 – 1910), a descendant of the house's original builder. James entered Virginia Military Institute as a cadet in 1860. Two years later, the young seventeen year old enlisted as a Confederate in the War Between the States. During a battle, James received a bullet wound to the head. He was wounded a second time, released from the army and returned home to Princess Anne County to spend the rest of his days at the Whitehurst family home. He was greatly affected by his wounds and was cared for by his sister (VMI archives, 1865). It is said that after his return from the war, his appearance frightened children. Being a lover of children, such rejection so emotionally wounded the man that, sadly, he henceforth retired to his house and refused to venture out. He finally died in the house.

Oral history has it that the ghost of Whitehurst preferred to manifest himself to children. When the Buffington's daughter Ann was still very young, she reportedly saw Mr. Whitehurst's white haired and bearded apparition in her upstairs bedroom. Standing in her crib, the toddler would frequently and excitedly point and exclaim to her mother, "Mom! Santa Claus!" while the family dogs barked in the direction she was pointing. Her delight was most probably shared by the long departed Mr. Whitehurst, as well, as he had been without the company of children in his latter years. On several occasions in later years, Ann Buffington and Martha Kellam (Stone), her best friend who often would sleep over for the night, awakened to find the bedroom's furniture rearranged (Stone, 2004).

The Kellams and Buffingtons were neighbors who enjoyed a long friendship that began when the girls were just toddlers barely out of diapers. Both girls were recipients of Mr. Whitehurst's benevolence and protection. The following tale chillingly illustrates how his ghost meant the children no harm. In fact, he seemed to guard them with fierce devotion. Keep in mind that this occurred in the more relaxed days when doors often remained unlocked and parents did not need to worry, as they do today, about the plethora of ills their children might encounter if left alone. This experience, as told by Martha, happened when she and Ann were ten or eleven years old.

First I have to tell you that in Ann's bedroom at the end of the upstairs hall was a fireplace, over which was displayed a pair of crossed Civil War era swords. Keep that in mind. One day she and I were by ourselves in the house, which wasn't the least unusual or unnerving for us under most circumstances. Well, this day we saw a man coming up the long lane in front of the house. We watched him through the window of the dining room, which is just below Ann's bedroom. As the stranger approached, we could see that he was kind of scruffy and odd looking. We were getting kind of scared. Suddenly, just as the man passed the circle of boxwoods on the lawn and got to the foot of the walkway that leads to the front door, a sword FLEW out of the window above us and landed point-down in the ground just a few feet in front of the stranger! The sword was still quivering as the man turned and ran off. For a minute, we just stared as the sword slowed and finally stopped vibrating. Finally realizing our danger had passed we cheered in appreciation and relief, "Yea Mr. Whitehurst!!! You saved us!!!" We checked the upstairs... no one was there.

The two girls grew up with a fondness for the ghost of Mr. Whitehurst, whom they considered their friend and protector. In contrast to the extreme unease expressed by the family maids, who never wanted to be alone in the house, the girls were not the least afraid and always felt safe at Longview (Stone, 2004). Martha shared that Mr. Whitehurst's interactions became fewer and farther between as the girls grew older. She agrees with local lore, which maintains that the man had a definite affinity for children, even in his after-life.

The two subsequent residents of the house never saw the ghost, but a guest of one claimed to have heard doors open and close when no one else was home. Both of the cats of the last residents would sometimes enter a room, stop abruptly, then turn and run in the opposite direction (Gilbert, 2003).

The house was built in about 1793 on land first owned by Francis Whitehurst who that year gave his plantation property of 150 acres to his son, Daniel (Kellum and Kellum, 1931). James Howard Whitehurst inherited 335 acres, known as the "Whitehurst Farm," in 1865 (PA County Deed book 47, p. 519). The house remained in the Whitehurst family until sometime in the 1930s. It has been called by various names with "Longview" being given by the Buffington family. One of the authors has spent many hours in the house and more than once stayed the night, but no ghost appeared.

The Whitehurst-Buffington Foundation received a 40 year lease for the house in 2012. For more information contact the foundation at P.O. Box 56114, Virginia Beach, VA 23456; Phone: (757) 427-1151.

A Pre-Dawn Encounter

My friends rented the Whitehurst/Longview/ Buffington House from the city for many years. Since it was so close to West Neck Creek and we were at the time training for a canoe race, we would often set off from there to go paddling before work. Early one morning in the darkness before dawn, while unloading a canoe from the top of my van, I heard a voice, walked to the front of the van and asked the person accompanying me what he had said. He said he hadn't said anything. I went back to untying the canoe's ropes and heard the voice again. "Did you hear that?" I asked. He answered that he thought it was me playing a joke. We were both a bit spooked, as we were both familiar with the ghost story and now we had both heard the weird voice.

We were certain what we'd heard was not normal, not human. We remained very still, trying to listen. Not hearing anything more and feeling a little foolish, we went about our task of lowering the boat. While carrying the boat into the dark woods where the small tributary joined the creek, a large owl noiselessly flew extremely close to us. Shaken a bit, but relieved to have a possible explanation, we decided that his was the "unearthly voice" we had heard say, "Whooo."

– Journal of Lillie Gilbert, 1986

Tombstone Returned Home

James Whitehurst's tombstone seems to have wanted to go home. Missing for years, it was during the first writing of this book found again. According to Ann Buffington, during her childhood the tombstone was located in the woods directly behind the Longview (previously, Whitehurst) house. David Kellam rediscovered the gravestone while roaming in the woods as a child, but when he returned to what he thought was the spot, the stone had mysteriously disappeared (Brown, 2004). As this book was first being written, the unset government CSA tombstone of James H. Whitehurst was again found somewhere in the

woods of the courthouse area countryside. Michael Rose, a member of Virginia Beach's Sons of Confederate Veterans Princess Anne Camp 484, was contacted for assistance. It is this group's duty to locate, reclaim and preserve veterans' gravesites. With the assistance of information from one of these authors as well as local history buffs with information on the Whitehurst family, and in honor of Mr. Whitehurst, the stone was placed in its rightful location on the premises of the old Whitehurst home.

Appearances and Disappearances at Lynnhaven House

You bet there are ghosts there.

~ Sarah Walke, 1972

uring a 1972 interview, previous Lynnhaven House dwellers Eliza and Sarah assured the newspaper reporter, "Yes ma'am indeed – you bet there are ghosts there." Mrs. Mary "Eliza" Smith had been a resident of the house from 1945 to 1950, whereas her sister-in-law Mrs. Sarah Walke lived in the house from 1939 to 1945 (Crist, 1972). Their families had worked on the farm of the Olivers, who later donated the house to The Association for the Preservation of Virginia Antiquities (APVA).

Said Sarah, more than once when the family was sitting downstairs they would hear footsteps of someone walking down the stairs from the second floor. She and her sister once saw a woman rocking in a rocking chair when they entered the house. The children only became alarmed and fled when they realized it was not their mother in the chair. When they intrepidly returned to the house for another look, the woman was gone. Sarah and her sister another time saw a little girl dressed in white standing in the hallway. The pale ghostly girl just "disappeared" (Crist, 1972).

Patrick McAtamney was probably only in about 8th grade when he and a friend decided and attempted to spend the night in the abandoned house:

> *It was just an old house, it was sitting back there, it was covered up with vines and brush. Nobody had any clue it had that kind of age on it, or maybe they didn't even*

care. It was all grown over, full of weeds, there were probably 20-30 junk cars around it. Nobody even thought twice about it. A friend of mine and I decided we were going to spend the night back there. For whatever reason, we decided we were going to do that. We had no business being back there in the first place. It was very dark back there ... there was a looooooong driveway going back there, for me as a kid.

It was really cold. Of course there was no light and you had to go through scrub and overgrown bushes even to get in the door. We were a little spooked, anyway. And we went upstairs, and we went in one of the upstairs bedrooms and it had wall-to-wall old newspapers, pieces of newspapers on the walls. So we peeled some of the newspapers off to make a little fire, just so we could see better and just for a little warmth. We couldn't keep a fire lit. We heard noises. We'd sit in that room and everytime we'd make a fire, it'd go out.

I forget what made us want to leave that room so bad ... but I remember we decided we needed to get up and out of that house. It had to do with noises. At that time [the house] had an enclosed stairwell and we came down the stairs and we had some little candle so we could see what we were doing, and as soon as we went out of the room to go down the stairs, some kind of blast of wind came – fvvvvvv – and blew that out. We came rrrrrunning out of that house.

McAtamney was not the only one who tried to brave the Lynnhaven House overnight. An Old Donation University student by the name of Jim who was responsible for much of the home's interior restoration during the early 1970s became convinced of ghosts himself when, while working alone, his tools would day to day be mysteriously moved from place to place. He also heard doors slam when alone in the house. The inquisitive young man decided to investigate further by spending the night at the place. He set up a cot and commenced his experiment but did not stay the duration of the night: he left after a few hours ... it got too cold, he claimed (Crist,

1972). Or, did the house get "too" something else?

Considered one of the best preserved of the early dwellings in the United States, the Lynnhaven House, built around 1725, is another historic property located along the Bayside History Trail in Virginia Beach, Virginia. This small brick house was once thought to have been built by the Wisharts, but it is now thought that its constructor was Francis Thelaball, who received 423 acres in 1685/86, on property adjacent to Wolf's Snare Creek (Nugent, 1992). Francis is also credited with a 1721 purchase of 250 acres of property where the Lynnhaven House stands (Turner, 1984), although no such transaction is listed in the Patent Book for that year.

Today, docents claim the Lynnhaven House is not the least bit haunted. The historic home has been restored by the Association for the Preservation of Virginia Antiquities. Today the house is operated with ongoing restoration by the City of Virginia Beach. Opened to the public in 1976, the house may be visited at 4409 Wishart Road, Virginia Beach, VA 23455. For additional information, call (757) 460-7109.

Rose Hall's
"Standing Jenny"

A noise of falling weights that never fell,
Weird whispers, bells that rang without a hand,
Door-handles turn'd when none was at the door,
And bolted doors that open'd of themselves...
And one betwixt the dark and light had seen
Her, bending by the cradle of her babe.

~ Lord Alfred Tennyson, *Night's Dream*

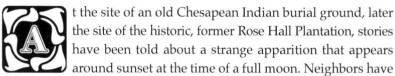 t the site of an old Chesapean Indian burial ground, later the site of the historic, former Rose Hall Plantation, stories have been told about a strange apparition that appears around sunset at the time of a full moon. Neighbors have told of what they describe as a young woman who slowly rises from the ground, then plummets into the earth of what they have assumed is her grave. She would do no harm ... just rise up from her burial plot and then disappear downward. She is known as "Standing Jenny." We are not sure why "Jenny" was given as her name, but the "Standing" part has an interesting local interpretation. Read on about the strange happenings at Rose Hall.

The property on which stood historic Rose Hall, a three-story farmhouse in Great Neck, was granted to colonist William Ellegood in the early 1700s. Even before that, an Indian village was in the vicinity. The original house, believed to have been brick with a gambrel roof, passed from the Ellegood family in 1804. It reportedly burned and the second house, built around 1820, was built a short distance from it. In its prime, Rose Hall's manor sat on 615 acres of farmland (Kellam, 1958). Swepson Brooks, senior warden of Eastern Shore Chapel for sixty years, ran the Rose Hall farm from the 1850s until his death in 1920. As steward of the church's communion silver, he hid it in a basket under his bed nightly and, during the Civil War, buried it beneath his setting hens in the chicken coop (Mansfield, 1989). Sadly, the house was razed in the spring of 2003. According to locals, there are legends of "Standing Jenny" having haunted the grounds of the old house. In one account, Jenny was an unfortunate young woman who died in childbirth sometime in the 1850s and was buried left in a squatting position. This Jenny was said to have roamed the halls of the Rose Hall house (Castleberry, 2003). Another story told to one of the authors is about Standing Jenny, the Indian Princess, who became ill with a very high fever. The illness took her life. As was the custom of the tribe, she was buried standing so that the fever could rise up out of her body with her spirit, both for her benefit in her next life form and for the protection of the rest of the tribe. Whichever tale of Standing Jenny holds the most truth, the area was reportedly once scanned with sonar equipment and a woman's skeletal remains were, indeed, found in the upright position (Nash, 2004).

Before Rose Hall was torn down, this same author was taken to the spot where Jenny was supposed to have been buried. There was no grave marker but someone had put a cement slab over the purported grave. The slab was not to be touched by machinery when the land was developed, but if you go there today it is gone, as is the tree that stood near by.

How much of the above is true, we may never know. As happens when progress and time take possession of and change markers and reminders, Jenny's story is fading away. Since Rose Hall was torn down there has been no sign of Jenny, or maybe no one remembers to look for her anymore. From a quote attributed to Captain John Smith, Virginia Indians' spirits traveled westward until they reached the setting sun. Has Jenny's spirit moved westward and is this why she has been seen at sunset?

While Rose Hall manor itself was not saved, many of its pine floorboards and bricks were put aside for use in renovation at Ferry Plantation House in the Bayside area of Virginia Beach. In the spring of 2004, the bricks were used for a walkway for Ferry Plantation House. Belinda Nash, a restorer, docent and long-time volunteer of Ferry Plantation said, "Rose Hall's heart will live on here" (Mizal-Archer, 2003).

Will Jenny live on as Rose Hall's ghost at Ferry, perhaps having relocated with her house's remnants? Only time will tell. If any of our readers has seen Standing Jenny, the authors would like to know of her whereabouts.

Rose Hall's bricks, before set as the walkway to Ferry Plantation House

Chapter 5

We Had Witches?!?

While we are the solitary prisoners of darkness,
the witch seats herself at the loom of thought,
and weaves strange figures into the web
that looks so familiar and ordinary
in the light of every-day.

~ "Witchcraft," *The North American Review*, 1868

Early Witches in Virginia

She is youthful or old as she pleases,
She sails the torn clouds in her barque,
The bright silver lady of midnight,
The crone who weaves spells in the dark.

~ Doreen Valiente, *The Witches' Creed*

uring the reign of James I of England (1603-1625), many people accused of witchcraft were "found guilty" and put to death. Witchcraft had been made a felony offense by English law in 1563. The early colonists of Elizabeth City Shire (County) in Virginia, part of which later became Virginia Beach, brought with them the laws of the British monarchy. These colonists, because they were English citizens, also brought their home country's superstitions, prejudices, and beliefs. The early court records indicate several trials and legal proceedings that the members of the Virginia Colony brought against each other. There was a heavy fine imposed against those making unjust claims, so the brave souls who actually pursued their beliefs into court cases must have had an earnest conviction that they were correct in thinking their neighbors to be involved in witchcraft.

There is no evidence that anyone was ever executed in Virginia for witchcraft. A Katherine Grady was said to have been hanged for witch-craft onboard a Virginia-bound ship, and authorities charged the ship's captain for her death once the ship arrived (Barden, 1992). Witch mania's resulting travesty of justice that occurred in Virginia pales in comparison to what occurred in 1692 in Salem,

Massachusetts, where twenty accused men and women were put to death. Witchcraft accusations in Southeast Virginia, however, preceded by several decades the hysteria that swept Salem.

An early record states:

> At a private court, held the 23d of May, 1655 at the house of Mr. Edward Hall in Linhaven. Whereas divers dangerous and scandalous speeches have been raised by some persons concerning several women in this county terming them to be witches, whereby their reputations have been much impaired, and their lives brought in question, (for avoyding the like offense) it is by this court ordered that what person shall hereafter raise any such scandal concerning any party whatsoever and shall not be able to prove the same, both upon oath, and by sufficient witness, such person so offending shall in the first place pay a thousand pounds of tobacco; and likewise be liable to further censure of the court.

Surely, the incredible fine of a thousand pounds of tobacco would be enough to keep frivolous accusations from coming to court. This gives a more than credible meaning to the term, "cash crop," as little in the way of hard currency was available and Virginia tobacco was used as money.

One of the core beliefs associated with witches was that they were Satan's minions, having entered into a contract with him. Witches were believed to have supernatural powers used to inflict harm on others and their property. It is difficult to comprehend that a person could be accused of bewitching a child to death or of riding a broomstick with another's sleeping husband aboard. Nevertheless, court cases of the county that was to become Virginia Beach were recorded about some who must have had such a strong belief that they accused their fellow settlers of witchcraft.

A court case filed 40 years after the mandate of 1655 upheld the tobacco payment, although the fine was reduced. In December of 1695 the county record states:

> Whereas Ann Godby, the wife of Tho. Godby, hath contrary to an order of the court bearing the date of May,

1655 concerning some slanders and scandals cast upon women under the notion of witches hath contemptuously acted in abusing and taking the good name and credit of Nico. Robinsons' wife, terming her as a witch, as by several depositions apears. It is therefore ordered that the said Tho. Godby shall pay three hundred pounds of tobacco and cask fine for her contempt of the mentioned order, (being the first time) and also pay and defray the cost of suit together with the witnesses charges at twenty pounds tobacco.

Another case involving Alice Cartwrite appeared in January 15, 1678:

Upon the petition and complaint of Jno. Sammon against Alice the wife of Thomas Cartwrite concerning the death of a child of the said Sammon who it is supposed was bewitched, it is ordered that the Sheriff do forthwith summon an able jury of women to attend the court tomorrow and search the said Alice according to the direction of the court." The search was apparently made to find any of a witch's marks on her body and the very next day, January 16th: "In the difference between Jno. Sammon plaintiff against Alice the wife of Thomas Cartwrite defendant, a jury of women (Mrs. Mary Chichester forewomen) being impaneled did in open court upon their oaths declare that they having diligently searched the body of said Alice, can find no suspicious marks whereby they can judge her to be a witch; but only what may and is usual on other women. It is therefore the judgement of the court and ordered that she be acquitted and her husband's bond given for her appearance to be given up."

Following Alice Cartwrite, there is apparently a twenty year gap in reporting as the next "witch" to be given court time was Anne Byrd. Accusations also extended to her husband, John Byrd.

At a court held the 8th day of July 1698, John Byrd and Anne his wife sueing Charles Kinsey in an action of defamation setting forth in their petition that the said

Kinsey had falsely and scandalously defamed them saying that the said Anne did ride him from his house to Elizabeth Russels, and that by such discourse she was reported and rendered to be a witch or some such like person, praying one hundred pounds damage with cost; the defendant for answer acknowledging that he had spoke words saying that he either dreamed or had such experiences. The whole matter being put to a jury who bring in their verdict as followeth: We of the jury do find for the defendant, Hugh Campbell foreman.

John and Anne had a busy day at the court as they also filed suit against John Pitts. Colonial beliefs in witchcraft aside, it is still remarkable that given the penalties for defamation, the local people persisted in their witch hunting.

Jno. Byrd and Anne his wife suing Jno. Pitts in an action of defamation setting forth by their petition that the defendant had falsely and scandalously defamed them, saying they had rid him along the sea side and home to his own house, by which kind of discourses they were reported and rendered as if they were witches or in league with the devil... The defendant for answer acknowledgeth that to his thoughts, apprehensions or best knowledge they did serve him so. The whole matter being put to a jury who bring in their verdict as followeth: We of the jury do find for the defendant.

While these cases have simply gathered dust and the names have been long forgotten, the famous Witch of Pungo is still remembered and fondly regarded by the present day residents of the city of Virginia Beach. Grace Sherwood, wife of carpenter and farmer James Sherwood, lived along Muddy Creek in the Pungo area and her troubles began a year earlier than those of John and Alice Cartwrite.

Legends of Grace

Only witches who rode on broomsticks to midnight meetings
could sail in egg-shells, and as witches cast spells
and exerted malignant influences on honest people,
it was plain that Grace Sherwood was a witch,
and ought to be tried and punished.

~ John Esten Cooke, 1884

race Sherwood was "different" from other county wives of her day: she knew too much about herbs and ointments; she wore men's clothing and worked in the fields beside her husband; she was perhaps too attractive. The wives whispered. Rumors and tales were spun like yarn off spinning wheels gone fast and wild. Hysteria was born of misunderstanding, jealousy and fear.

Some of the bizarre tales were formal charges against Grace, documented and preserved in old court records of the day. Certainly some of these were nightmares, maybe even in hysteria believed by the accuser and told as truth. Others stories were passed through the oral grapevine, persisting well past Grace's death. The following legends of Grace Sherwood are summaries of those written by Louisa Venable Kyle in her time-treasured book, *The Witch of Pungo* (1973), as well as those gleaned from court records and the research of Jimmy Moreland (1988).

In the course of what had been a quiet farm life in the lovely countryside of Pungo, Grace, in her mid forties, became the target of witch mania. When victims of an unfortunate but natural event or sheer bad luck, her neighbors felt cursed and pointed their blaming fingers toward the purported witch. Among their accusations, they formally claimed in court that Grace had caused both blight to their crops and disease and death to their livestock. The woman, they thought, would dance around their cows, bewitching them to produce sour milk. In one nightmarish court record entry, one woman even claimed the "witch" had entered and exited her home through her door's keyholes as a black cat accompanied by a man with the head of a goat. Amazingly, Grace was said to have mounted and ridden the woman like a horse.

Hysteria spread like an untreated rash. Grace was feared and socially spurned. When outright denied an invitation to a picnic on the shores of the Currituck Sound, legend says that she, in today's terms, crashed the party. Passing by the picnickers in an eggshell boat, she tied her fragile craft to a nearby tree by a thread and then ate her lunch under a tree, mocking the onlookers in laughter.

Many times Grace was charged and had to defend herself in court. Sometimes, she countercharged her accusers. While in jail awaiting trial for witchcraft, some believed she was each night unfettered by the devil himself and the two would fly to the scene of the future ducking, where they danced on the shore in defiance until dawn. Grace was returned in early morning to her prison cell where she stayed until the next evening, when the pair repeated their performance. As the tale goes, to this day nothing grows on the spot on which they danced.

Another incredible eggshell story is told about Grace making herself very small and sailing to the British Isles. Arriving in England, she picked a bit of the herb, rosemary, and then sailed back to Virginia in her eggshell boat. All of the rosemary that grows in today's Virginia Beach is said to have come from this delicate culinary mission of Grace.

In another story, Grace was said to have tried to trick the sheriff into releasing her by convincing him to let her show him something novel. When he reluctantly agreed, Grace sent a young lad to a tavern with the directive to return with two unwashed pewter plates. Well, the mischievous lad dipped the plates into a rain barrel before delivering them to the imprisoned woman. But he was not to fool Grace: she banged the plates against the boy's head and sent him straight back to the tavern for two different plates, admonishing him not to dip them in a rain barrel this time. With the new plates, Grace talked the sheriff into letting her outside to show him the marvel at hand. Once outside, she placed a plate under each armpit, flapped her arms, and flew up and away.

While we know Grace was imprisoned after her infamous trial by water, some folk versions of the ducking event maintain that, when cast into the Lynnhaven, the clever woman escaped prison by disappearing into the air or out into the Chesapeake Bay in (you guessed it) an eggshell. In another tale, she failed the ducking test but revenged her onlookers by assuring that they, too, got drenched. After her ducking, she haughtily promised them a worse ducking than hers. You see, once back on shore, she was said to have summoned and unleashed a great thundercloud. As the jury and witnesses to her trial ran for cover from the torrents of rain, they could hear Grace's loud cackling laughter even over the thunderclaps.

Even though Grace died a natural death 34 years after her ordeal, her legacy continued: even her death has its story. It is said that while she lay by her fireplace dying, a gust of wind came down the chimney and filled the room with a cloud of ashes, which, when settled, displayed a cloven hoof print at the hearth. Grace herself was gone. In another story, seven days of rain followed her burial, causing her coffin to float up out of the ground, much as she had resurfaced from the river at her ducking. Her sons drained the coffin of its water and reburied her. The next day a neighbor saw the coffin again out of the ground, with a black cat perched atop. As the story goes, the men of Pungo were immediately alerted and they set out to shoot every cat in sight.

"Duck the Witch, Duck the Witch!"

Few more disgraceful scenes were ever enacted in the prosecutions
for witchcraft, either in Connecticut or Massachusetts,
than this which took place in Virginia…

~ Samuel G. Drake, *Annals of Witchcraft in New England*
and Elsewhere in the United States, 1869

itchduck Road, Witchduck Bay, Witchduck Bay Court, Witch Point Trail, Sherwood Lane, and Witch Gate are the names of some streets in Virginia Beach, Virginia that were adopted from the infamous "witch" trial that took place there in 1706. The area was once traveled by hundreds of settlers. Colonists lined the banks of the river, many of whom took part in the trial by water of Mistress Grace Sherwood, accused of witchcraft.

Today, more than 300 years after Grace's trial, one hears the tales that echo the shoreline. When the wind is high and waves are lashing the shore, some hear the chanting … voices of the crowd… the words are not clear but muffled; they have been described as words of an angry crowd. Then again, it could be Mother Nature playing tricks with one's ears.

The twinkling of firelight is said to be seen night after night in the heat of the summer sky. Is this the lantern of Grace Sherwood seen in

the distance? It has been said that she returns to the point and dances with the devil himself. Perhaps not just the common firefly, these could be the eyes of ghost hunters searching for her return. This light, seen on several occasions from the fifth to the tenth of July each year, is larger than most. How do we explain this? Or do we dare try? The people who live in this area have grown to accept strange happenings: windows  vibrating, furniture moving, a haunting laugh in the darkness. The part that gets their attention is a cold chill on the warmest night at the time that the voices are heard.

It was an overcast, chilly day when Grace Sherwood made history at Witchduck Point, two hundred yards out into the water. Accused of witchcraft, she was given the old English ducking test: cross-bound, if she were to sink and drown, she was innocent; if she were to float and swim, the pure water was casting out her evil spirit and she would be guilty of witchcraft. Grace had a no-win situation. The woman swam, thereby confirming she was witch. On shore after her ducking, a group of "ancient and knowing women" then subjected poor Grace to a humiliating search for telling signs of witchcraft on her body. Such signs included "teats [for the devil's suckling] spotts and marks about her body not usuall on others." Who, indeed, would have passed the scrutiny of these no-doubt biased, overzealous women? On Grace, they found two suspicious marks, providing the jury with further confirmation of her guilt. She was jailed and when released, returned to her home in Pungo to live a quiet life and die a natural death in the year 1740 at the age of 80.

As many believe, Grace returns to the place of her trial. She has every right to. This woman before her time just knew too much: a healer, user of herbs, and a midwife, she tried to help her neighbors as well as their animals. She raised three sons after her husband's death, tended her farm of one hundred and ninety-five acres, and lived through the trial by water at age forty-six. Could you, at age forty-six, live through this ordeal and then spend your days in a timbered jail with a straw bed on which to sleep? Could you return to your home with no ill feelings towards those neighbors who had caused this to happen?

Grace has every right to her legacy and the places that were named after her conviction. If you should see the twinkling of the firelight across the water as if a lantern were dancing, just let it be. Share your story with others, as Grace has a story to tell. Maybe this way her legend will never be lost.

> *"Out on her!* screamed the elders,
> And they all rose up as one;
> Then again they cried through the chill night-tide,
> *There is godly work to be done!"*
>
> ~ Clinton Scollard, 1903

In June of each year, "Gracie's Girls," two troops of Girl Scouts, clean the statue at Witchduck Road and Independence Boulevard.

Warding Off Witches

he Witch Ball, dating back to medieval times, was traditionally hung in the window to ward off witch spells, evil spirits, and ill fortune. Purportedly, there are three theories behind this idea. The first maintains that the witch was scared by her own reflection in the glass, which, being round, worked on witches approaching from any direction. Second, because of the clarity of lead crystal glass, the ball's beauty casts sunrays on one's walls, preventing a witch from entering one's

dwelling. The other belief was that hanging the decorative balls in the window tantalized evil spirits thought to be threatening a home's tranquility. The evil spirit, mesmerized by the ball's reflective beauty, would touch the sphere and thereby become absorbed and trapped in the web-like strands of glass inside the ball. One would not dare to break a witch ball, as one would never want to risk releasing the inestimable evil spirits trapped within its beauty.

Fishermen, being very superstitious in early days, would use the same glass balls as floats on their fishing nets. Harboring beliefs in sea devils and sea spirits, they would take the witch balls from the home to protect their nets and catch. In certain cultures today they are still used for the same superstitious reason.

Bottles were another witch repellent also made by glass blowers of the early 1600s. The witch bottle trade was a unique one. With his hollow tube the craftsman would transform sand and other silicates under intense heat causing the properties to solidify from the molten state without crystallization. With the hollow rod, taking great care not to inhale, he would blow this molten glass into a sphere and then work his magic to mold it into the bottle. This transformation in itself gave great respect to the bottle as it transformed to a holding vessel. It was the belief of the early colonists that one should plant this hand blown vessel at the threshold of the door of one's dwelling to ward off witches or demons. In this bottle one would place a brass pin, an iron nail, a piece of lead and the urine of the owner of the home the bottle was to guard. A cork was then placed in the bottle and it was turned cork-end down and buried in the earth outside the door. Did the witch bottle ritual keep the evil spirits away? One could not say, but while doing several digs in the area of Kings Grant and Witchduck Point, archeologist Floyd Painter found several of the blown bottles unbroken. With Grace Sherwood's trial by water that took place on July 10, 1706 in the waters around these two developments, it is safe to say that the early settlers believed quite strongly in this practice.

Rosemary, the herb of remembrance, is a Mediterranean shrub. Philippa of Hainault, wife of Edward the III, first grew it in England in the 14th century. Then it was used as an excellent tonic, as it was regarded as being uplifting and energizing.

Rosemary plants in Virginia Beach, Virginia have been believed to have the powers of Grace Sherwood behind them. While the legend says that it was brought by Grace from the shores of the Mediterranean in an eggshell to transplant in the new colony of Virginia, an overnight voyage across the ocean is quite the feat for even a so-called witch! More probably the woman transplanted cuttings of the herb that her mother had brought from the old  country. Folklore aside, by historical accounts it seems that rosemary has grown in Virginia since the late 1600s.

If Grace Sherwood was the herbalist and healer that she was supposed to have been, she apparently used rosemary as a cure for practically everything. As oral tradition has it, herbalists used rosemary's fresh pulverized needled stem to extract the essential oil to make a stimulating rub for arthritic conditions, rubbed the oil into the temples of those with headaches, and used the dry aerial parts to make a fine tea, its hot infusion helpful for colds, sore throats, indigestion, fatigue and headaches. Lastly, Grace would have known to soak a compress in the hot infusion for sprains, alternating every three minutes with a cold rosemary compress.

One can imagine the trouble a healer could get into in those days with herbs in their repertoire. If the herbal treatments proved helpful in alleviating sickness or fevers, to the untrained or ignorant witness, it could be interpreted that Grace had the Devil himself to help her. In actuality, Grace was a healer taught by her mother. With all of the good that she might have accomplished, because of misunderstandings and fear born of ignorance, she was accused of witchcraft, tried by water and convicted on July 10, 1706.

If thou be feeble boyle the leaves in cleane water and washe thyself and thou shalt be shiny…smell it oft and it shall keep thee youngly.

~ Banckes' Herbal, 1525

Ghosts versus Spirits

According to renowned parapsychologist Hans Holzer (1997), ghosts and spirits are entirely different entities. Ghosts are the auras or souls that have passed out of persons' physical bodies. Earthbound, they remain at or near their place of passing due to emotional ties or trauma. Unaware of their own passing, ghosts are troubled or tormented souls who obsess with their unfinished business. They are incapable of reasoning for themselves or taking much action. Thus, they are usually harmless.

Spirits, on the other hand, are the surviving personalities of persons who have "passed through the door of death in a relatively normal fashion" (Holzer, 1997). Unlike ghosts, maintains Holzer, spirits can continue a full existence "in the next dimension" and "can think, reason, feel, and act." They retain their memories, interests, and their abilities to convey these to others. These are "free spirits" who can travel, follow people, and appear at more than one place. Spirits are often attracted to one place or person or another by emotional reasons; they often have a desire to communicate.

The Sherwood Spirit

The foolish reject what they see and not what they think;
the wise reject what they think and not what they see.

~ Huang Po

sn't it befitting that a house on Witchduck Point be deemed haunted ... or, more appropriately, bewitched ... perhaps by Grace Sherwood herself? In 1972, the Retired Commander Robert E. Mann and his wife moved into the house they had built on North Witchduck Road. According to daughter Leslie Mann Workman (2003), she wasn't before then a believer of paranormal activity and apparitions, ghosts or poltergeists. Soon after moving in, however, she and her parents became acquainted with what they are certain is the spirit of Grace Sherwood. As the years went on, Grace seemed to become fond and even protective of the family members.

Of spirit Grace's antics and activities, Leslie summarized, "She loves to hide personal possessions of persons living in the home. Those belongings can always be found in the back bedroom upstairs. She paces in the attic above the two upstairs bedrooms most nights. She has shown herself when asked. She is very protective over the ones who live in that house whom she loves. As for those who do not understand what is happening in the house, they move, and quickly I might add."

Leslie shared several detailed recollections of her family's earliest encounters with the famous Witch of Pungo. "On Christmas Eve of 1974, my mother woke up to find Grace sitting in the chair in her bedroom saying something she couldn't hear. She was only showing herself from the waist up." Leslie then described an incident that well illustrates Grace's protectiveness of her mother. Mrs. Mann was out of town in September of 1978, on Leslie's 21st birthday. Leslie and others were in the house's family room. "We were making fun of my mom when the wall-anchored mirror in front of the front door fell off the wall, MISSED the antique table and shattered glass everywhere. At the same time the light in the hall of the laundry room fell out of the ceiling and glass shattered everywhere. Both exits to the home were blocked by shattered glass," she said. Not to be left out, the family's "Grandmother" clock joined in the commotion and stopped her hands dead at 6:30 p.m. Leslie, having learned a lesson, added: "We quit talking about my mom!"

The clock, by the way, could not be coaxed to keep the time again. Over two years later, at exactly 3 o'clock in the morning, she finally ceased her silence and started her on-the-hour chime. Recalled Leslie, "By the time the first bong denoting the hour hit, we were all at the bottom of the stairs. It chimed exactly three times and hasn't stopped working since!" Grace, she believes, had finally forgiven the transgression.

The spirit of Grace is not housebound, as is your garden-variety ghost. She doesn't always stay at the house on North Witchduck, and she has been apt to go with family members when and where she wants. Leslie explains of Grace, "Oh, she can leave, and has, when she desires." The following anecdote describes how Grace one time vacationed with Leslie and her friend:

> My best friend, Karen, and I were going to Cape Hatteras for the weekend to surf and scope out the boys. We stayed up most of the night making chocolate chip cookies. We started talking about Grace. Lo and behold, she walked by. Karen had a cow and wanted to go home. She ended up staying. On the way down we were so cold in the car, despite that it had no air conditioning! It was so strange; we knew she was there. We stopped for gas and cigs and stuff and when we got back to the car, items had been rearranged in the back seat so as to make an area for someone to sit in, but we couldn't see anyone. It was SO freaky. At the hotel, the bedspreads were "cheesy" and if you touched them, they instantly wrinkled. I'm a neat freak and insisted that the beds be made every time we left the room. We came back to the room on the first day and, I swear my hand to the heavens and God above, you could

SEE where someone had laid down on my bed! This happened Saturday, Sunday and Monday. Karen and I could never, to this day, figure out how someone could lay on my bed where they did without making wrinkles in that stupid material. I know that this sounds nuts but I swear Grace had to have floated down on the bed; it's the only way.

Grace has had further travels than her jaunt to Cape Hatteras. When Leslie left home in 1979 and moved to New York, the spirit-witch accompanied her for nearly a month: Leslie knew Grace was there. The very day Leslie finally didn't feel so desperately homesick that she thought she could actually stay in New York and make a life, Grace left New York and returned to the house in Virginia Beach on North Witchduck Road.

When Leslie moved back to Virginia Beach in 1983 into a brand new custom-built home on Front Royal Road, Grace was there. There was a loft that overlooked the formal living room and made noise when you walked on it. Leslie complained of it to the builder, but to no avail: no one could make the loft stop creaking when Grace paced it at night. Leslie's then-husband took a night job, which left her alone at night with her one and two-year-old sons. Leslie stated she felt protected by Grace every night he was gone.

Leslie and her boys later moved to a townhouse in another area of Virginia Beach. She was a single mom then and her work schedule was erratic. She started getting phone calls at all hours with immediate hang-ups. This went on for weeks and no one could do anything about it. One evening, Leslie returned to the townhouse late. While carrying one of her sleepy boys to his bed, she felt a resistance: "it was like my house didn't want me in it." When she went and got her other son, it finally struck her that something was wrong in the home. She walked down the hall and turned on the light in the living room, only to find that the place had been totally ransacked. It turned out that vandals had broken in, watched TV, eaten the family's food, stolen food and other items, and slashed all the furniture. "It was horrible," recalled Leslie, "It was so bad."

Before the police arrived, Leslie looked down the hall from the living room straight to her bedroom and saw Grace, standing above the carpet with her arms outstretched in a consoling manner. Said Leslie, "Oh, how I wished she could have held me. I was so scared and was feeling so alone until I saw her." Grace remained with Leslie until her parents, who then lived in Florida, arrived to assist their daughter.

After a near fatal car accident in 1986, Leslie moved to Florida to be near her parents. She asserts that Grace has been in her parents' house in St. Petersburg, as well as her own house, a few blocks away.

Since her family vacated the house on North Witchduck Road in 1980, Leslie has interviewed three families that have lived in the home. "There hasn't been an owner that I have met who, after I introduce myself and tell them my parents had the house built, doesn't let me in. I always ask them, 'So, anything unexplained going on inside you want to talk about?' Gets me in every time." During her last interview of 1996, she took over 48 pictures of the house, both inside and out. The first four pictures on the roll, of her children, came out nicely… but nothing else, no pictures of the home, developed. Said Workman, "The second roll, the same thing… the last picture came out, nothing from the home developed."

Leslie fully intends to buy the home on North Witchduck Road one day and live in it again. At this time in her life, however, family priorities keep her in Florida. Said Leslie of Grace, "I feel her twice a year: September 12th and December 24th. Grace Sherwood has been in my life from the moment we moved into that home on North Witchduck Road in 1972 and I pray she never leaves me."

Annie the Conjurer

That old black magic has me in its spell.

~ Johnny Mercer

s imparted by local historian, Edna Marie Hendrix, the following comes to us as a truth-told community legend. The Afro-American heritage of our area had links to the "other world" by conjurers. By definition a conjurer is one who can summon spirits by magic. It was the duty of these folk heroes to perform feats not only of medical prowess, but to deal with "other world" problems in the community by help from the spirits who could be called in to perform their particular magic. It had been 117 years since a person accused of witch-like crimes was brought before a judicial group in Princess Anne County. In 1923 Annie Taylor, a strong personality beloved for her skills, was condemned by a group of non-believers and banished from the county and the people she served.

During the early 1900s Princess Anne County did not have a colored doctor. Many colored residents went to Norfolk for their medical needs. Other colored residents relied on Annie Taylor, aged and wrinkled colored "cunger" of Norfolk, Virginia. Short and thin with a full head of gray hair wrapped in cloth, eyes that pierced the soul, and a personality that drew you to her like a magnet, she traveled to farms and homes offering her unique ways of healing.

According to oral history, as Annie Taylor knelt on her knees, others could see the spirits rise up and out of her. She said on several occasions, "On my knees I can feel your pain. My ghost stands ready: bring me a witch pig." Eyes ablaze, this woman cured their chills, fever and other physical ailments. On the other hand, it is said she made white landowners in Princess Anne County very ill when she visited their farms.

In 1922, Annie felt the need to sit under a large tree in the Colored Cemetery located near Old Donation Church. Tears streaming from her eyes, she mumbled about "hanging trees" and setting free both colored and white folks' ghosts. It is said that later that day headstones fell in Old Donation Church Cemetery and the Colored Cemetery.

On December 3, 1923 a warrant for the arrest of Annie Taylor stated her crime as: "Trespass on the farm of C.C. Hudgins, and practice of Cunger treatment against the peace and dignity of the Commonwealth" (File Box #517, 1924). The court records stated that more than sixty colored tenants had paid Annie Taylor for her services with pigs, chickens, and geese, some of which were stolen from Hudgins' farm.

[Annie had been conjuring on the 350-acre farm of Christopher Columbus "Lum" Hudgins (Federal Census 1920, 1930). His farmhouse, still standing and known by most as the Pembroke Manor House, dates back to the 1760s. A striking historical fact is that Hudgins' farm, where the occurrence took place, is not far from the spot where Grace Sherwood was ducked for witchcraft in 1706 in the chilly waters of the Lynnhaven River.]

After learning of the facts involved, John J. Tilton, a prominent white lawyer of Norfolk who served as attorney for Annie Taylor, and Magistrate J. Frank Bell of Princess Anne County, together delivered a severe lecture to the tenants on the farm of C.C. Hudgins regarding their beliefs in witchcraft. Charged with conjuring for colored tenants, receiving stolen goods and performing witchcraft on the Hudgins farm, Annie was convicted of a misdemeanor. She was also ordered to leave Princess Anne County, with the promise of a year of imprisonment if she returned.

Chapter 6

Haunts
of
Private
Residences

We have no title-deeds to houses or lands,
Owners and occupants of earlier dates
From graves forgotten stretch their dusty hands
And hold in mortmain still their old estates.

~ Henry Wadsworth Longfellow, *Haunted Houses*

Eerie Electronics at Fairfield

The fence around a cemetery is foolish,
for those inside can't get out and those outside don't want to get in.
~ Arthur Brisbane

he house at Fairfield had been on the market for two years with only one bite. When the prospective buyers discovered there was a cemetery in the backyard, they quickly changed their minds. In 1994, enter Charlene. She was very taken with the home, but once she stepped into the backyard and saw the lovely live oak, she fell in love with the place. She was told about the cemetery several times before she made an offer on the house. Undeterred, she bought the place. Charlene has always said, "I bought the tree and the house came with it."

She moved into the house. During the arduous task of unpacking, Charlene received a lot of telephone calls and, upon answering, even on the first ring, heard nothing but silence or the occasional crackling noise. These annoying calls would come at all hours of the day and night. Charlene unpacked and plugged in more telephones as well as an answering machine. Then, something even stranger began to happen: only one of the three telephones would ring, and it was not always the same telephone... they seemed to take turns! Additionally, Charlene could call out from her telephones, but it seemed no one could call in.

Charlene's friends complained that she was never home and did not have an answering machine. She checked to make sure her friends were calling the correct telephone number. They were. Even after several service calls, the telephone company could find nothing wrong with the lines either in or outside of the house.

After months of such communication calamity, Charlene finally in desperation went to her backyard and sat under the canopy of the ancient live oak in the middle of what she understood to be the old graveyard. She had decided to have a little talk with "whomever" might hear her. She explained that she had the full intention of living the rest of her years in her house... with or without telephones! She further asserted that if there were intentions of running her off, "they" had "another thing coming!" After that talk, Charlene never had another problem with her telephones.

Charlene then became intrigued about the cemetery, and began to ask questions. She found out she was living on land that was part of the old Fairfield Plantation, and her cemetery was the family plot of the plantation's Walke family. Sometime in the past, she was told, the cemetery's headstones had been moved by the Princess Anne Garden Club to the cemetery at Old Donation Episcopal Church. The remains remained.

Now if it was only that easy to discover the secrets of the large live oak tree in the backyard. Charlene had been told the Fairfield oak was estimated to be 300 to 500 years old and that it had been known as a hanging tree. The oral history of trees such as this is provocative but difficult to verify. If indeed a hanging tree, Charlene wondered, was it for the Walke family's use? Or was it for the use of nearby communities and towns?

Next in the series of unexplained electronic events, the following occurred. The microwave, coffeepot, and toaster would turn on by themselves when no one was in the kitchen, or when in use, would turn off before finishing their jobs. This time Charlene did not bother to investigate reasonable causes for these curious happenings. She immediately returned to the backyard's cemetery, sat down, and again explained that she meant no harm and was here to stay. After that, all eerie electronic mishaps ceased.

Now of course, older houses have wiring problems. With many of the lines running underground, things can happen to cause electrical surges and bad telephone reception. But then again... what do you think?

The Fairfield Plantation was a sprawling, baronial "village" style land estate belonging to Anthony Walke I, the first of several of his name to settle in Lynnhaven Parish in the 17th and 18th centuries. His father, the mariner Thomas Walke, rich in land and wealth, was the first Walke to arrive in Virginia from Barbados.

The Fairfield Oak: Authenticated in the book, *Remarkable Trees of Virginia* by Nancy Ross Hugo and Jeff Kirwin (2008)

The Kenstock Manor Mystery

All houses wherein men have lived and died
Are haunted houses.
Through the open doors
The harmless phantoms on their errands glide,
With feet that make no sound on the floors.

~ Henry Wadsworth Longfellow, *Haunted Houses*

his is the story of a woman's dream house that became her own, complete with its tales of a former resident's suicide and a resident ghost. Years ago while at a yard sale in the Kenstock neighborhood off Great Neck Road, Juanita Graziadei fell in love with the old farmhouse tucked in amongst the newer homes. Several years later, it came to her attention that the charming house was up for sale. She was delighted. The Graziadeis swiftly made the purchase and the Kenstock house became their home.

Tales of hauntings conveyed with the real estate, shared Juanita, but she initially just chalked these up as typical stories concocted and perpetuated by children whose stomping grounds contain an old, vacant house. Kenstock was supposedly "haunted" by one resident who lived there only about a year and then committed suicide.

Even before the purchase of the house, Jim Graziadei was witness to a strange occurrence. When he was viewing the house one day, his visit coincided with another realtor's showing of it. The potential homebuyer with the realtor was quite upset, as she had just seen what she described as an apparition. After the Graziadeis had signed a contract on the house, this woman's husband filled Jim in: his wife, he said, had seen a ghost sitting on the washing machine. One rumor has it that the kitchen with its laundry area was the scene of the reported suicide hanging. Indeed, the Kenstock ghost tends to center its activities in this part of the house.

Through the years, Jim Graziadei and the couple's oldest son have had a few uncanny experiences in their house. Juanita had one possible sighting, herself. One night when her husband was out, she went to sleep alone. She awoke in the middle of the night, for no apparent reason. Sitting up in bed, Juanita spotted the vague figure of a man standing in the hall outside the open bedroom door. As she was asking herself if she was awake or asleep, the figure vanished (Graziadei, 2003).

"I'm not into the whole spirit thing," Jim reported, "but just odd stuff goes on. No rattling of chains or anything like that and no ghost has held a knife to our throats. If there is a ghost, he's friendly." Perhaps the friendly spirit of Kenstock manor is partial to sunlight or light. "Stuff gets moved around and lights that were turned off at night will be on the next morning. We'll pull down the shades, close the curtains and the next morning, the shades are up and the curtains are pulled back" (Graziadei, 2004).

While an untimely, violent death, especially by suicide, may suggest the source of a haunting to many of us, the identity of Kenstock's ghost seems to have a rival. Said Robin McElhaney (2003), whose family owned the farmhouse for many years, "When my family had the house everyone who died here died of old age." She admits that her Aunt Harriet Ailstock, who was owner in residence from the 1950s until her death in 1985, was eccentric enough to perhaps remain in the home in her hereafter. The woman, who had never married, had been the nursing superintendent of the Virginia Beach Hospital. The house passed out of McElhaney's family after Harriet's death.

According to world-renowned parapsychologist Han Holzer's take on hauntings, one may be missing the mark by searching for a violent death in a house's past to validate its ghost. Considering Holzer's position as he reported in an interview with Rev. Laurie Sue Brockway in 1998 (originally published in *New York Spirit* magazine), Aunt Harriet should not so easily be discounted as the ghost in question:

> *The ghost personality is generally in various stages of psychotic condition — otherwise they would move on. The stay behind is someone who lived in one place for a very long time, and usually dies a gentle death; they just fall asleep, no violence, no pain. They are unused to any other place... Low and behold, at death, they're still where they were before. The physical body isn't there — but there's a body and they see themselves, so they stay put. That's why people go to the funeral of Aunt Minnie, come back and there she is in her usual chair.*

Kenstock is one of Virginia Beach's few remaining old homes of the 19th century maintained by private residents. The three-porched cedar shake house built in the late 1850s has a hipped roof and unusual ornamental features such as lidded dormer windows and a half-moon window. An iron crenulation adorns the roofline; its roof is shingled with Vermont six-sided slate (Barrow, 1997). The interior boasts a large center hall and four parlors with corner fireplaces downstairs, five bedrooms upstairs.

The name "Kenstock" came many years after the house was built. It is a combination of the co-owners' names, Herman Kennedy, of Georgia, and James "Walter" Ailstock, of West Virginia, who jointly bought the house as a summer home sometime in the 1930s. In its prime after its purchase, Kenstock Farm was a 63-acre agricultural tract that extended from Great Neck Road to the banks of Wolfsnare Creek (McElhaney, 2003).

A Very Old Woman

~ William Stanley Braithwaite, 1920

She passes by though long ago
Time drained the life out of her tread;
She died then, yet she does not know
That she is dead.

Her footsteps are indefinite
With sound, and who are dead should pass
Sandaled as the wind when it
Moves through the grass.

Her shadow twitches on the walk,
And who are not of life should run
Shadowless as a lily's stalk
In full day's sun.

Yet these cling to her—stricken sound
And shadow casting ragged stains;
They drag behind her on the ground
Like broken chains.

It is silence mastering her tread,
Darkness, insidious and slow,
Blotting her imprint ... but she is dead
And does not know.

Mysterious Happenings at Laurel Cove

As I was going up the stair,
I met a man who was not there.
He was not there again today,
Oh, how I wish he'd go away.

~ Hughes Mearns, 1875-1965

ne of the most actively spirited homes in Virginia Beach, surprisingly, was built in 1972. When a young family moved into their new Colonial-style home across from an old graveyard in Laurel Cove, they barely got settled in before unsettling events got under way. Unexplained noises included those of footsteps, doors opening and closing, a consistent 6 o'clock doorbell ring, knocks, bumps, the rustle of skirts, moans, groans, giggles, and even talking. Voices called, "Help me." One night, the couple was awakened to the sound of what seemed to be a party downstairs in their living room, complete with music, laughter, and the voices of men and women conversing (Ashley, 1977).

Disturbances were not limited to noises: things were not just heard, they were felt and moved. Beds shook. A large picture and a vase were found, as if thrown, on the den floor. "Something" took the hairpins out of a guest's chignon; perhaps the same "something," with an attraction to women's tresses, repeatedly stroked the woman of the house's blonde bangs. During a party, a plate of food mysteriously drifted from a guest's lap and up into the air, landing several feet away with food intact. Another time, a full cup of tea turned upside down without spilling a drop. Still another time, a candle flame from a chafing dish mysteriously shot up several feet in the air.

As for visual evidence of the extraordinary, the Laurel Cove family's co-residents often left their mark by way of handprints and footprints.

Prints of a child's hand and six-toed foot mysteriously appeared one day on the master bedroom's mirror (Bonko, 1973). A child's handprints later materialized on the oven door and the glass panes of a cabinet. Oddly, these marks defied being photographed, just as noises and interviews often eluded being audiotaped. The man of the house witnessed apparitions running the gamut from a strange glow (one once followed him up the stairs) to the actual gliding form of a woman who sat down and spoke to him.

It didn't take long for the family to become convinced that a whole slew of ghosts were co-residing in their then-modern abode. In spite of numerous spooky events, through the years they came to lose their fear: no one, after all, was ever really harmed. In fact, the "spirits" may have been protective of the family. For example, when the man of the house once became imbalanced backward at the top of the stairs, "something" pushed him forward and prevented his fall.

Susan Scheier Scott, a teenager living in Norfolk in the early 1970s, skipped school one day to accompany her girlfriend on an interview with the Laurel Cove family. It is her recollection that the research was for a school project. Susie, both enthralled and scared witless, was witness to the aforementioned imprints of a child's hand and six-toed foot, both eerily imprinted on the mirror in the master bedroom. While she does not recall many other details of the visit, this she clearly remembers: on the drive home, when the two teens rewound the audiotape to replay the eerie interview, the tape was empty. Nothing. Absolutely blank (Scott, 2003).

Larry Bonko of the *Ledger-Star* was among the group who met in the home with a medium in November of 1973 for a chilling "séance" of sorts in the house's kitchen. He reported an uncanny coldness settled in the room as the séance got underway. The medium entered a trance-like state and answered the others' questions, sobbing, from the perspective of a 27-year-old "Rosemary Savage." When asked why she was crying, she responded, "Because I am dead;" she did not know how she had died, but sobbed repeatedly, "You don't listen to me" (Ashley, 1977).

The family also sought the assistance of Charles Thomas Cayce from the Association for Research and Enlightenment (A.R.E.). He was said to have recommended that the woman of the house begin recording her dreams and that she also have a Catholic friend of hers say a prayer and sprinkle holy water. Paranormal activities abated only temporarily after these interventions (Ashley, 1977).

The family continued to seek assistance. A psychic who visited the home immediately developed a severe headache and began correspondence with a "spirit" named George Williamson. George claimed he and his family, wife Ella Mae and daughter Mary Bee, were tenants who had died in the house in a fire. Mary Bee, shared George, was fascinated with the coif of the woman of the house, and was responsible for stroking her hair. Upon further questioning, George maintained that the baby with six toes was his brother's little boy. The psychic later visited the upstairs master bedroom where she reportedly saw a little girl playing in the closet (Ashley, 1977).

The family who first lived in the haunted house in Laurel Cove has long since moved on. While many residents of the neighborhood have heard the story, most do not know the exact location of the house on which to pin the tale. That there used to be an old cemetery in the neighborhood is (or will be) news to most. It is unknown if the Laurel Cove residence continues to host ghosts.

A Cold Room
on Newtown Road

Not far from the gurgling reaches of the Great Dismal Swamp somewhere within the deep recesses of Virginia Beach's lost lagoons sits this turn-of-the-century tribute to paradise lost, now with its stately facade from another place in time crumbling from the nearby swamp's murky, bubbling presence. This is a place where noisy scientific experiments and glass-shattering explosions from inside the house are usually followed with maniacal laughter. Who knows what's hiding in the bushes outside.

~ Jerry Harrell, 1970s

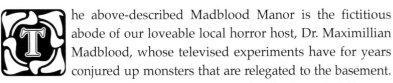 he above-described Madblood Manor is the fictitious abode of our loveable local horror host, Dr. Maximillian Madblood, whose televised experiments have for years conjured up monsters that are relegated to the basement. Dr. Madblood, portrayed by Jerry Harrell, has had a cult following since his debut on the air in 1975. While Madblood Manor was fabricated, Jerry shared that he has been in a real haunted house. His story is as follows.

From 1976 until the original series went off the air in 1982, Doctor Madblood and the gang were involved in the annual March of Dimes Haunted Houses. John McClung, who was the head of MOD at that time, invited us to come and help design the displays and the tours.

Each year a house that was empty and/or had been scheduled for destruction was donated to the charity and for two months, a team of volunteers would take over the house and construct the show. With the help of experts like Bobby Melati and his crew of lighting and technical wizards, these were easily the most elaborate haunted house events ever put on in this area.

In 1977, the house that was chosen was on Newtown Road. It stood where the on-ramp to I-264 from Newtown Road is today. It was a small two-story house and had been scheduled for demolition later that year. After we got into the house and started planning our displays, I began to hear stories about how the house was haunted. When I asked about this, I was told that a little girl had died in one of the upstairs bedrooms and that her spirit still inhabited the room. The proof of this was supposed to be in the fact that this room was always cold. And I do mean cold. Even with the windows sealed and no ventilation, this room was in fact much colder than anywhere else in the house. ... cold enough that even on warm October evenings, you could always see your breath.

We discussed this with the March of Dimes folks and everyone agreed that we would not incorporate this into our presentation, as it involved an actual family tragedy, and would be inappropriate for our purposes. Instead, we used a fog machine to lay a carpet of mist in the room, painted the ceiling with day-glo stars and told our visitors they were in a landing area for spacecraft, which led to the next room that was supposed to be the spacecraft interior. (This was the year of Close Encounters of the Third Kind.) The landing area was cold and very quiet.

Other than the "cold room" there were no other manifestations of ghostly activity, although a number of the volunteers (many of whom did not know the history of the house) reported feeling "weird" in that room.

The 1977 Haunted House was one of the most successful ever staged. When it was over and we were packing up to leave, I remember one of the volunteers thanking our young hostess for letting us use her dwelling. Within two months, the house was indeed demolished.

The Implausible in Pembroke

Have you ever noticed there is never any third act to a nightmare? They bring you to a climax of terror and then leave you there.

~ Max Beerbohm

llen, (not her real name) has rented her house in the Pembroke Manor neighborhood of Virginia Beach since 1983. To this day, she has no idea why eerie events would occur in the less-than-historic structure. The only possible clues to the occurrences may be an old fenced graveyard that nestles on nearby property and, of course, that the house sits on land that was once part of the large Pembroke estate. Its manor house, still standing in the neighborhood, dates back to 1764. For whatever reason, Ellen and her children, now grown, have experienced many an implausible event in their otherwise unassuming residence.

The strange occurrences seem to be tied to holidays, especially Christmas, and center in certain rooms in the house in which more activity occurs. What would start as an occasional oddity that would make Ellen question her own reasoning eventually escalated to surreal, downright creepy experiences that would make her hair stand on end.

Imagine Ellen's horror when a small toy vehicle with battery-run headlights turned the corner from the dining room and entered the room where she was sitting. Not once but twice this happened, with no prior sound of the car falling off or otherwise being moved from its usual place on the shelf. The car, which she keeps for the use of her grandchildren, can only make turns with the physical assistance of a person... or, of a.... whatever. This so spooked Ellen that she removed the batteries from the toy, an action that thankfully halted its "unmanned" maneuvers.

Then there was the day that Ellen felt a yank on her hand as she was braiding her long hair. The hair tie she was holding was snatched from her hand, disappeared, and has not been seen since. This was not the only physical manifestation of the "ghosts." Ellen has been hit by a presence, but not in the usual sense … the blows caused a burning sensation, but the resulting marks were quite superficial.

Ellen has had reason to be concerned about the safety of herself and her family. One time, something told her to go check on her sleeping grandchild. The child was ice cold. Alarmed, Ellen picked up her granddaughter, took her to the living room, and warmed her up. In a disturbing photograph of someone holding this same grandchild, shared Ellen, "you could see these 'things' all around her." On occasion, forms have lingered above Ellen and her son in their respective beds, rendering them helpless in what she thought were attempts at suffocation. "It made you frozen, as if 'it' took control and you couldn't think," she explained. One might surmise that the feeling she described may have been, if not a presence's attempts to smother the occupants, symptoms of shock. Such an occurrence, after all, would surely frighten the average person witless!

Apparitions have appeared to Ellen on several occasions. Usually, these took form from what initially looked much like clouds or smoke. A figure, if one can call it that, has been seen marching quickly and madly around the house.

Ellen's son seems to have been a target of many of the ghosts' manifestations. Ellen didn't think much about his claims of hearing voices through a fan until she one day heard them herself. "It was a horrifying, eerie sound, " she offered with an audible shiver in her own voice. This was not the only occasion in which voices were heard. When Ellen replayed a tape of her daughter Teresa singing a song, a voice that was not heard during the recording clearly said, "Get out, Teresa; get out." When Ellen would leave town, family or friends who stayed at the house would invariably hear loud banging on the walls. "Maybe they missed me," Ellen joked. The report of the bangings indicated to Ellen that the house's hauntings were not targeted to her family, alone.

Nonetheless, Ellen feels she has a gift of seeing and feeling things that others cannot always see and feel: not a gift, she says, that she always wants. Her unwelcome houseguests, she believes, are evil, perhaps demonic forces. About this unwanted sixth sense, Ellen says, "I can [sense and feel things] if I want to but I try not to... you're so alone with it."

What did Ellen do about these frightening events in her home? While she never sought the help of an expert in the field of the paranormal, she did mention the situation to people at her church. Unfortunately, they offered her weird looks instead of the help she had hoped for. By way of her own defense, Ellen has more than once tried confrontation as a means of ridding the house of the pesky presences. She is not sure if her false bravado and loud assertions of "If you're here, leave me alone!" worked a charm, but she has also threatened the ghost(s). Using prayer coupled with a very assertive voice, she seems to sometimes temporarily banish the mysterious beings. Ellen maintains she also uses mental blocking or simply goes to sleep to get "out of" experiencing these eerie presences.

One time while praying for their ghosts to go, Ellen and her daughter witnessed six or more little cloudy lights hover and then float up and out through the ceiling of the room. At the same time, the typically cold room became warm. It was their hope that the ghosts had left once and for all, but they hadn't, as other events occurred after the incident.

Hauntings, however, have dwindled significantly in the Pembroke house. Ellen now feels she has made peace, in some way, with whatever it is that shares or shared her living space. Her future plans are to move to another home in the city, but not because of the hauntings. Something has changed and she has not recently suffered the touches, sights or sounds of what she hopes is now an "unhaunted" house. "I feel safe now," she explained. She added, "I feel I can let someone else have the house."

Footsteps at Lake Shores

On the threshold swift I pause
Sound of ghostly footsteps awes

~ George Sylvester Viereck, 1907

er husband's military assignment brought Jane Reed and her family from England to Virginia Beach, VA. Their temporary home was easy enough to find: they took the same rental that their friends, who had just returned to England, had vacated.

The Reeds temporarily lived in the house at Lake Shores for six months before moving to their next residence. "The house always had a strange feeling. I never, ever was happy there," Jane recalled about their Lake Shores abode. "The place was spooky," she added. While she never saw anything out of the ordinary in the brick bungalow, she did sense a presence, often feeling that there was someone else there when, in fact, she was (by common standards) alone. But she did hear things.

"At night, I used to hear people walking around on the wooden floorboards," Jane shared. When her husband was out of town, not once did she sleep through the night easily, without waking. When she once mentioned the mysterious footsteps to her husband, who tends to be less prone to such feelings and experiences, Jane said, "He'd actually heard those sounds too and, thinking it was the boys, had even once gotten up to check, but no one was there."

But the most chilling experience happened in the daytime, when Jane was alone in the house. She was sitting on the sofa in the living room, talking to her sister on the phone, when all of a sudden she heard and felt pounding footsteps run straight up to her, then stop abruptly. She gasped and broke off mid-sentence, prompting her sister to ask, "What's wrong?" When Jane told her what had just happened, her sister, who was privy to Jane's feelings about the house, exclaimed, "Oh my gosh!"

Jane inquired of her friends, the previous renters, about the house's uncanny atmosphere, but they had not had similar uneasy feelings about the place. However, they did share something about the house's owner, who lived there prior to their rental, which may shed at least dim light on Jane's experiences or, at the very least, prompt some conjecture. It seems the owner, during his residence, had quite a collection of human bones in the house, among which was a skull. If there were displaced spirits, this house may have had its share. It was even said that the man had an up-ended coffin in a corner, for display (Reed, 2004). More than enough for conjecture, wouldn't you say?

Chapter 7

Spirits Without Walls

Whence and what are thou, execrable shape?

~ John Milton, *Paradise Lost*

Eerie Events on Elbow Road

The world is lost…Majestic portals close
Upon me. Sombre pines keep watch and ward
Within this temple of sublime repose.
A redwing blackbird lifts a muted chord
In praise of silence. Shadowed in the lake
All ecstasy, all pain and longing seem
To mingle. Here at last may mortals slake
Their thirst for waters of immortal dream.

~ Mary Sinton Leitch, 1937

haded by an overhead thick-knit canopy of trees, Elbow Road winds through a dark and damp forest. Just beyond the deep ditches that are the narrow road's non-shoulders, one can spy smooth aging knees of cypress jutting upward from still, night-black waters. Straggles of gray Spanish moss drape the tangled underbrush.

Serene… or spooky? Read on and then decide.

A woman as well as a little girl, both of whom supposedly met with tragic ends, are said to haunt Elbow Road. The woman is said to have once lived along the road. As local legend goes, she was murdered and her body was never recovered. Purportedly, lights turn on and off in the location of her house, despite there being no building on the site now.

Legends floating around further contend that at a certain curve on Elbow Road, if you sit very still and quiet at midnight, small, child-size footprints start to appear, as if someone was walking toward you. This is supposedly the ghost of a little girl who drowned in Stumpy Lake one day when fishing with her father.

Teens who have visited Elbow Road in search of ghostly encounters are of the belief that one must touch the water in order for an apparition, one of the above or another, to make its appearance.

Brenda Reid, who grew up on Elbow Road, shared the following childhood memory. Late one night, there was a knock on her door. A young female employee of a nearby convenience store had apparently accepted a ride home from a male customer after her shift was over. On dark Elbow Road, the driver pulled the car over at the "spillway," the area of the road where a dam has been built to accommodate runoff water from Stumpy Lake. After they had stopped, the man attempted to assault his passenger. The girl, terrified, ran from the car and jumped into shallow Stumpy Lake to escape the assailant. As she took her plunge, she cut herself on debris on the lake bottom. The driver, fearing someone would hear her screams, fled the scene.

Seemingly out of nowhere, a hand reached out to help the young woman out of the oil-black lake. She struggled out of the water, grateful for the assistance. Her immediate response to the confusion and fear was to run. Cut, scraped and bleeding, she made it to the nearest house, which happened to be the Reids'. She banged on their door, desperate for assistance.

Brenda, only about thirteen or so at the time, remembers her parents wrapping the wet and bleeding woman in a sheet. She remembers the story, as relayed above. But what is prominently etched in Brenda's memory is this portion of the story: after her attacker had sped away, the young woman never even got a

glimpse of whomever had helped her out of the water (Reid, 2003). The mystery Samaritan has never been identified or found, nor were there any footprints at the lakeside but those of the woman.

With its darkness, ditches, and twists, Elbow Road has seen more than its share of tragic accidents and has indeed been the depository for several murder victims throughout the years. This alone is enough fodder to feed anyone's ghostly imaginations.

Elbow Road, under study for improvement, was at the time of this publication a two-way corridor that cut through wetlands linking Virginia Beach and Chesapeake. The descriptions listed here were written before the pending widening or straightening of the old roadway, which has shown on maps as far back as the 1890s. Today, the lake and 1500 acres surrounding it are part of the City of Virginia Beach's Stumpy Lake Natural Area. Part of the acreage includes daylight walking trails into the beautiful wilderness setting. The 270-acre lake is bordered in part by a 72 par public golf course, hardly the setting for ghostly happenings of the past.

Frightening Events at False Cape

Ghosts at False Cape? Yeah, we've got ghosts.

~ Brad Mitchell, 2004

n order to entertain the possibility of ghosts roaming the terrain at False Cape, one should appreciate the area's history. False Cape in southern Virginia Beach, formed by a mile-wide barrier spit between Back Bay and the Atlantic Ocean, long ago earned a reputation as a ships' graveyard. In fact, the cape has long conspired with the Atlantic Ocean to keep the pristine coastal area of beach, dune, marsh, and forest as uninhabited as possible by humankind. For its part, the landmass, when viewed from the Atlantic, mimics Cape Henry in its appearance. In doing so, much like a wolf in sheepskin it lured unwitting victims, in this case ships, into its lair: hence, the name "False Cape," thusly dubbed in the 1800s. Once the ships were enticed into the shoal waters by the cape's trickery, their fates were sealed.

It is said that survivors of such a shipwreck developed Wash Woods, one of the area's first communities, in the mid to late 1800s. Wash Woods, an interesting name born from less than charming circumstances, was a thriving little community around the turn of the 20th century. Located on False Cape behind a barrier dune line facing the Atlantic Ocean and subject to the whims of nature, the community was made up of hardy souls who made a living farming, fishing, trading, and scavenging lumber or products from ships that became beached or damaged during storms. The derivation of the name Wash Woods has been said to be either for the ocean waves that would wash over the dune line and into the woods during storms or from the fact that wood would wash ashore. Indeed, ghost-like stumps, contorted and weatherworn, protrude from the stretch of

sand at low tide ... like the ill-fated passing ships of yesteryear, also victims of the rising and falling sea.

Remains of the Clythia, sunk January 22, 1894 when she went ashore two miles north of Wash Woods Life-Saving Station

Another explanation for the name Wash Woods may have come from a sailing ship in distress. Lumber or salvage from ships that grounded was more than a serendipitous find. Claimed by the area's inhabitants, the lumber was frugally used to build houses and churches. In 1895 a three-masted schooner, the *John S. Woods*, washed ashore. The terrible storm that caused it to become aground caused great concern for fear of losing the crew. For three days attempts were made to rescue the sailors. Finally on the third day, the men of the nearby lifesaving station managed to get a lifeline to the ship. Because of their efforts, no lives were lost, but the ship could not be saved. The *John S. Woods* broke into pieces and the valuable cargo spread itself upon the beach.

This ship was carrying lumber and it is this wood that was used to build the Methodist church, called The Little Chapel in the Woods (Lukei, undated document). That the lumber was cypress was all the more valuable to the residents because of the rot and insect resistant qualities of

that particular tree. Before this church was built, the members of the community had to travel to Knotts Island to worship.

The community eventually grew into a small town, hunting and fishing being the primary pursuits of its residents. The people were resilient and hardy, used to their small strip of land being washed by storms, but after devastating flooding during the 1920s many left. A decided blow came in 1933 when a killer hurricane hit the east coast. After this disaster, most residents abandoned their village; the shifting sands that gradually covered their dwellings eventually forced others out. After a nearly three-month freeze of Back Bay in the winter of 1936, "the spectre of hunger stalked through the small community," leaving nine of the twelve remaining families in "acute distress." With the assistance of the Coast Guard for transportation, the Red Cross provided assistance to these needy families (*Virginia Beach News*, 1936).

With its profuse seasonal waterfowl population, False Cape was infused with hunt clubs and their clubhouses, some swanky and others not, from the turn of the century through the 1960s. With the exception of the depression years, wealthy local and out of state businessmen escaped city life to visit the private gunning clubs that provided access to the plentiful ducks and geese found on the Bay. As a source of revenue, several Wash Woods residents served as waterfowl guides to these northern sportsmen (Jordan & Jordan, 1975). But even so, full-time residents of the area remained few after the mid 1930s.

If nature's slow push to move residents out wasn't enough, the ferocious Ash Wednesday storm of 1962 put one of the final nails on the coffin of the Wash Woods village, leaving little remnants of this courageous little community today except a part of the old shingled wooden steeple from the church, some foundation bricks, and a little graveyard. The mute testimony of the voting records of 1968 proved at least eleven

Dear Ingrid,

I see the dead people here, dancing the disappearing dance. They fade in and out, smiling amid the trees and shadows... Before they died they would've scoffed at their peculiar little dance, but the dead people have learned that it's only the little things that matter. Is this you? Are you among the dancers? Are you watching me? The ghost of a woman sleeps high up over a church steeple. She awakens, floats down from above and whispers in my ear: "Don't give up - you are right on the verge of your dreams."

Ellen
Wash Woods

POSTCARD

PLACE
STAMP
HERE

people still had property here as they cast their ballots supporting the Democratic candidate. This last election was held in John Waterfield's house at the False Cape Gun Club (Tyler, 2004). These were indeed some of the last public residents of False Cape's Wash Woods. In 1968, the State of Virginia began to purchase properties and the area became False Cape State Park. Today, only a few park employees live nearby the obsolete community of Wash Woods.

False Cape is indeed a unique setting for strange and varied happenings. Read on.

The Little Chapel in the Woods

The Night Visitor at Barbour Hill

Deep into that darkness peering, long I stood there wondering, fearing...

~ Edgar Allan Poe, *The Raven*

Cam is not the type to conjure up spooks. In fact, she prides herself as being a sensible woman, quite independent, quite used to managing on her own. She had already lived in Virginia's woods at Staunton River and again at Kiptopeke, both times serving as a state park's assistant manager. Of course, those assignments had placed her closer in vicinity to other park personnel. Here, at False Cape, the park's other two employees lived with their wives nine miles away. Not even shouting distance.

Cam and her two little boys were assigned to live in the park's small house at Barbour Hill. The house is fronted and shaded by majestic live oaks, their old limbs reaching every which way. The soft sandy soil blanketed with oak leaves borders the house. Nearby are wooded marshes and relic dunes. A stray tombstone or two from residents of yesteryear are scattered throughout. Comfortable enough. Desolate, but peaceful.

Cam had hardly been at Barbour Hill a week. It was a hot August night. The air conditioner was running to ward off the stifling, balmy heat. She had put the boys to bed and had later gone to bed herself.

Suddenly, Cam woke from a sound sleep. No noise woke her ... she'd not heard a thing. Rather, it was the uncanny feeling that she was being watched. Much to her horror, at the window through the blinds she spotted the silhouette of a figure. He appeared to be a man, hair shaved close to his head.

The dark figure moved about as she watched frozen in terror.

When the figure had gone, Cam mustered up enough courage to search the outside premises, armed with a baseball bat. Nothing. No footprints, no car tracks... besides, visitors of the park have to hike, bike, or boat in. Cam found not one sign of anyone having been there. She immediately called the other two staffers, one of whom came to her place to help look around and calm her down. Although slightly relieved, she didn't sleep a wink after the incident. The next day as they were discussing the nerve-racking incident, the other rangers were truly doubtful that Cam had really had a night visitor. They laughingly suggested to their "green" co-worker that it was just the jitters of being in a new location, so far from anyone else. Hearing her story, the authors are convinced that Cam saw something, as is she.

The Crying Child of False Cape

With its history of tragedy, death, and desertion, it is no wonder that False Cape State Park is the wide, outdoor cradle of a crying child. Today's visitors to the 4,321-acre park are likely cautioned to beware of ticks and other biting insects, poison ivy, and the poisonous cottonmouth moccasin snake, but they may or may not be forewarned of the eerie, high-pitched sound that may pierce their ears at night.

Stephanie Herron is among those who have heard the poor, bewailing child:

> *In 1999 myself and four other Wild River Outfitters employees were down at False Cape State Park to teach a "Sea Kayak Discovery Weekend" - a wonderful event filled with kayaking, good food, and environmental education. It was just before dawn and I was sleeping on the low trundle bed in the front room of the old hunt club… the best spot in the house as far as I am concerned, probably because the many windows allow the serenity of Back Bay to flow in and wrap you up like a soft summer blanket. Vickie Shufer, a naturalist interpreter, was sleeping in the bed next to me.*
>
> *My sleep was easily disturbed that night from the grunts, snorts and various rustlings of the 19 others in the house. Therefore I really didn't think it was too strange when I heard the high tinny cry of a baby. I thought to my sleepy self, "sounds carry easily over water, the park ranger and his wife must have a baby."*
>
> *"Maa Maa," it cried pitifully. I remember feeling sorry for the child, the crying just sounded so mournful.*
>
> *When I got up that morning I asked Vickie if the ranger had a baby and if she had heard it crying earlier. She confirmed that the ranger did not have a baby. "But I have heard the baby crying before. Once I was awakened in the middle of the night by a baby crying. I listened to it for several minutes, realizing there was no baby in the house. The thought went through my mind that these were just vibrations and that I could either lay there and listen*

*to the baby crying or I could roll over and go back to sleep.
I chose to go back to sleep."*

Authors' note: The "vibrations" spoken of here refer to a phenomenon that Mary Summer Rain discusses in her book, *Phantoms Afoot* (1993). It is her belief that in situations where death occurs with incredible trauma, a vibrational imprint is left in the area that replays at certain times. Certain people can "pick up" the feelings and sounds from such tragic events. Along the same lines, parapsychology expert Dr. Hans Holzer talks of "psychic impressions," replays of past highly emotional events "impressed into the atmosphere of the place or house" (Holzer, 1997). These replays, he says, are hard to differentiate from real ghost encounters and probably account for the majority of sightings. Holzer maintains that any sensitive person can pick up on and "re-experience" these impressions to some degree or another.

When the occasional camper in False Cape has inquired about the childlike crying, the park's assistant manager provided reassurance by offering up bobcats as the culprit... but she is unsure if the felines are, indeed, the offenders. "Who knows?" she said to the authors with a shrug of uncertainty. "It *could* be bobcats" (Barnas, 2004).

If not a bobcat, what is the crying sound in the park that has been heard by many? Is this a child, long gone from this world, whose ghost returns to cry for help, or from fear, pain, grief, or desperation? Did someone's son or daughter long ago stand on deck of an offshore ship in the bedlam of a storm and cry for a parent, just before being washed overboard and into a watery grave by a relentless wave? Or did a child survive a shipwreck and wander the beach in search of his or her mother, who had drowned and was never to be found? Perhaps this is a child who suffered hardships dealt by nature, or who was a victim of a hunting accident in the

area's days of prolific birding. Maybe the child ghost visits the nearby Wash Woods cemetery and bemoans the loss of a loved one.

False Cape State Park

For those wishing to experience this unusual and beautiful place, information about the park is available on the website, www.dcr.virginia.gov/state_parks/fal.shtml. Access to the park is through the Back Bay National Wildlife Refuge but no public motorized land vehicles are permitted. The interior trail is closed during the migratory waterfowl period of November 1 through March 31. The mailing address is 4001 Sandpiper Road, Virginia Beach, VA 23456, Phone: (757) 426-7128. Primitive camping is allowable year-round: for reservations call (800) 933-PARK. Day visitors can tour a portion of the park through an hour round-trip tram ride operated by the Back Bay Restoration Foundation. Tram inquiries should be directed to (757) 619-6429. Tram trips leave from Little Island City Park at the south end of Sandbridge Beach and start on April 1.

Chapter 8

Rappings & Rogues

Poltergeist phenomena are generally supposed
by the skeptical to be the work of artful
and mischievous children . . .
But in many cases which seem to have been carefully observed and
reported the physical effects are
of a nature quite incompatible with child agency.
A child may produce strange noises or throw an
occasional stone, but the movement of heavy furniture,
or the flinging of missiles, which enter a room
from outside when the child is in the room and actually under
observation cannot be explained in that way.

~ Herbert Thurston, *Ghosts and Poltergeists*, 1953

Three Hangings
at Lynnhaven Bay

*You must leave him hanging in a good strong
Chaine or Rope until they rott and fall away.*

~ Sheriff of Elizabeth City County, 1700

egend has it that the notorious Blackbeard hid along the cove-pocked Lynnhaven Bay in the colony that would become the state of Virginia. In fact, Blackbeard Hill on the shores of Lynnhaven Bay near Cape Henry in Virginia Beach was supposedly named as pirate Edward Teach's sentinels used its summit from which to scan the bay for prey. No one today is exactly sure where this lofty dune was located, but some believe it may be the old sandbank still standing some fifty feet or more above sea level within First Landing State Park, on its south side of Shore Drive (*The Beach*, 1996). It is still said that, on a clear night when conditions are right, the notorious swashbuckler's gun is heard ringing through the calm air.

Blackbeard was killed in North Carolina in November of 1718 by an expedition of men from Virginia sent there for that very purpose. It was then the tradition, some say by order of Governor Spotswood, that executed pirates be hanged by chains near harbor entrances and left there as warnings to other pirates who might potentially wreak their havoc in the same waters. In fact, Blackbeard Point at the confluence of the Hampton and James Rivers was named so, it is said, because the skull of Edward Teach* himself for years hung there on a pole. Legend and oral history further maintain that part of this very skull was later fashioned into a silver-plated container that served as a large drinking vessel or ladle.

Historians have put to rest many former beliefs of barbarous Blackbeard's activities in the immediate vicinity of what is now

Virginia Beach, Virginia. Even if these waters cannot claim fame as the primary so-called "stomping-waters" of Blackbeard, they were, indeed, so infested with pirates during this Golden Age of Piracy that a council met in 1699 and ordered the militias of the area, including that of Princess Anne, to provide lookouts along the shores. If lookouts spotted any suspicions of pirates, they were to notify the militia immediately (Turner, 1984).

One year from this decree, it was not Blackbeard's but another pirate's treachery that took place in Princess Anne County, Virginia. Like Blackbeard's tale, this one ends gruesomely on a pole (actually, three poles). It was April of 1700. Post-event depositions sworn before the court and recorded in "Survey Report No. 4385, 13 May 1700" during these pirates' trial provide an interesting depiction of the encounter.

It was the French pirate Lewis Guitarr who, over a number of weeks, had captured a total of five ships, all but one outward bound from Virginia, in our very own Lynnhaven Bay. He had taken some prisoners and confined these in the hold of his ship, called the *La Paix* (ironically meaning "The Peace"). As pirates were wont to do, Guitarr had acquired booty in the form of tobacco and other goods from the merchant ships.

Word of Guitarr's exploits in the Lynnhaven Bay got to the Governor General of Virginia, and action was taken. The 30-gunned *H.M.S. Shoreham*, employed to protect merchant vessels in the rogue-infested waters of the day, set out and engaged the pirate ship in battle. Pirate Guitarr fought under a blood red flag in a skirmish that lasted six to eight hours. The *La Paix* came out worse for the wear and tear, with 39 of her crew killed. Alas, she ran aground at Lynnhaven when her lines were shot away.

As the story then goes, Guitarr surrendered but not without first striking a bargain: he asserted to the Governor that he would blow up his own ship, with its English prisoners in the hold, if he and his pirates aboard the *La Paix* were to be slated for immediate execution. True to their word, the pirates were imprisoned, not executed, in Hampton and ultimately sent back to England. But the day of the battle between the *Shoreham* and *La Paix*, one pirate by the name of Houghlin had swum ashore and was captured, and two others named Franc and Delaunee were found on the captured merchant vessels. As at the time of Guitarr's surrender these three had not been aboard the *La Paix*, the Governor figured they, technically, were not subject to the terms of the agreement and could therefore be made an example of. Therefore, the three pirates were sentenced to be hanged.

Per custom, the hangings were to take place on or near the site of where the crimes had been committed. The following warrant for execution, "all and every of these directions" to be observed, was sent to the court of Princess Anne County, Virginia sealed the 17th day of May, 1700:

> You are to cause 3 Gibbetts to be erected in Your County, of Ceedar, or other lasting wood, one at Ye Cape, one where John Houghlin was taken and one near where the Pirates first engaged her Majesites Shipp, the Shoreham, which you may easily find out by inquirey. In which Gibbetts You are to cause Severall Pyrates herewith sent to be hanged up, vizt: ffrancis Delaunee at the Capes, Cornelius ffrank at the place where the Pyrates Shipp first engaged her Majesties Shipp, the Shoreham, and Houghlin at the place where he was taken. You must leave him hanging in a good strong Chaine or Rope until they rott and fall away.

Surely the hangings were well attended by residents of the county. One can only surmise that the pirates' corpses hung for a very long time in their fated spots as they served to ward off other plunderings by rogues of the seas.

* Blackbeard's given name may not have been Teach at all. A look at source material from documents printed during his lifetime reveal his name to have been spelled "Thatch" or "Thach" or "Thache" (Moore, 2004). See next page:

...so our Heroe, Captain Thatch, assumed the Cognomen of Black-beard, from that large Quantity of Hair, which like a frightful Meteor, covered his whole Face, and frightn'd America, more than any Comet that has appear'd there a long Time. This Beard was black, which he suffered to grow of an extravagant Length; as to Breadth, it came up to his Eyes; he was accustomed to twist it with Ribbons, in small Tails, after the Manner of our Remellies Wigs, and turn them about his Ears: In time of Action, he wore a Sling over his Shoulders, with three brace of Pistols, hanging in Holsters like Bandaliers; he wore a Fur-Cap, and stuck a lighted Match on each Side, under it, which appearing on each side his Face, his Eyes naturally looking Fierce and Wild, made him altogether such a Figure, that Imagination cannot form an idea of a Fury, from Hell, to look more frightful.

~ Captain Charles Johnson, *The General History of the Pyrates*, 1724

Blind Stone and Burroughs

The Invisible Force, a ghost of most extraordinary tastes,
holds dominion in this little corner of Princess Anne County,
the county where spirits have walked
since time almost immemorial.

~ E.W. Burroughs, "A Strange Story of Stranger Happenings,"
The Invisible Forces, 1953

Two good friends, one a bit older than the other, planned a sleepover, the first for each. The two boys settled in for the night on the ground floor of the two-story house. With the sun having set, lights off and the house dark, the boys grew weary of talking and drifted off to sleep. The father of one had placed sleeping pads on the floor for them and provided a pillow and blanket for each. Out of the blue, "Plunk," one boy's head hit the wooden floor as his pillow was jerked from under his head. "Hey," we can imagine that one saying, "Why'd you do that? Give it back!"

The other responds, "What? I didn't do anything!"

"Yes, you did. You took my pillow." "Did not."

"Did so!" And so on.

Pretty soon all the tussling and arguing awakened the dad who came downstairs to see what the fuss was about. A typical night's sleepover, you ask? Not quite. As the first boy was accusing the second of stealing his pillow, the other's pillow rose in the air and tossed itself across the room. This little incident was the start of many strange unexplainable events that haunted the two for the rest of their lives, at least when they were together.

The year was prior to 1906 and the subjects of this incredible story, Eugene Woodland Burroughs and Henry Stone, were neighbor boys of families in a small community called Sigma in what was then a very rural Princess Anne County. The father, Mr. Burroughs, heard the boys' story and told them offhandedly that it must be the Invisible Forces at play: while he was referring to a former resident who had lived and died in the house over a hundred years past, he had in fact coined the term for what was to become an amazing, perplexing phenomenon between his son and Blind Stone for many years to come. "Blind" Stone was so called as he had lost his sight at age nine from an accidental gunshot.

As it turned out, the Invisible Forces would frequently manifest themselves, primarily through kinetic mischief, when the two friends were together. Blind Stone and Burroughs were as puzzled and frightened as any onlooker when unusual things, apparently prompted by some chemistry between the two, would be set into motion.

Burroughs eventually moved to Norfolk and became an electrician with the Norfolk Navy Yard. Stone remained in Princess Anne County and managed a fishing business, despite his visual disability. Regardless of the physical distance and lengthy travel time between the two, for about a forty-year span the men would still get together. Most often a curious audience was in attendance as word quickly spread about the inexplicable events the friends' co-presence provoked. No one knew what to expect when Blind Stone and Burroughs were brought together for what came to be called "sittings," but one could usually count on something happening and few left disappointed... scared witless maybe, but not disappointed.

During a sitting, all would take seats in a locked room in a circle and wait for events to begin. The Invisible Force would often and suddenly throw grown men, chairs and all, into a tangled heap on the floor. Not to be spared, Blind Stone and Burroughs were among those tossed. Pictures would come off the wall and float around in the air, sometimes landing light as a feather to the surprise of the startled visitor who would suddenly notice something growing ever so slightly heavier in his lap. On one occasion, barrels of whiskey moved around the room. Covers flew off beds; coats and suitcases marched mid-air into the room. In fact, all kinds of items would take to the air and prance around.

Skeptics and scoffers were among those who came to witness the goings on between the two men, aptly referred to by *Beacon* writer Mary Reid Barrow as the "psychic twosome" (Barrow, 1993). Blind Stone and Burroughs were not permitted to sit side-by-side and those who suspected trickery were known to even hold the men's feet and hands during the sittings. As the manifestations did not abate and word of the strange events spread afar over the years, a Dr. Byrd with the *Scientific American* came to investigate for a period of about two weeks. His report indicated that he had seen but not understood and could not explain the mysterious happenings (Burroughs, 1953).

Many people had experienced some of the eerie events that took place over the lifetime of the two friends. The first reporter to write about Stone and Burroughs was Charles W. Houston of *Norfolk's Virginian-Pilot* on June 27, 1926. His testimony follows:

I felt his ghostly, icy breath upon my cheek; I was manhandled by some curious force; I saw eerie manifestations of a weird force, subtle beyond detection by ordinary human nature; I heard many strange and unearthly noises and saw curious things done, but candidly, I don't believe it because I don't believe in ghosts spirits or spooks.

But, believe it or not – I will tell just what happened while I, with a dozen or so others, sat in a little room in a little farmhouse near Sigma, on Seaside Neck, Princess Anne County, with two men whose presence together in a single darkened room gives rise to mysterious movements of material things.

Pictures floated about the room, bed clothing from an adjacent room floated in, men were hurled, together with their chairs, to the center of the room, a door opened, apparently unaided, and other things calculated to raise the hair of brave men and to throw fear and trembling into the hearts of the staunchest were done.

The principals – or mediums, if you please – are just plain ordinary citizens, friends since boyhood, who are as much puzzled over the force they seem, in small measure, to control, as are the most astounded witnesses. And they declare they are themselves awed by the force they have seen in operation so many times through 30 years.

Curious things have been done before, and have been written about, but Friday night was the first time that "The Invisible Force" – ghost, spook spirit, ectoplasm or whatever it may be – has ever done his stuff for a representative of the press. Although those who had seen it before declared the sitting Friday night was a tame affair comparatively, it held enough thrills to last one ordinary human being just one lifetime and three-quarters. I'd like to see it again, and I hope I may be spared to do just that thing, even if the price may be the exchanging of my raven locks for a shock of snow-white hair.

Oh-h-h-ho! Whew! Gosh! Oh! Then to the tune of weird rapping, your hair stands on end and you wish you were a thousand miles away. A moment later when your shattered nerves recondition themselves, you want a neighbor with his flashlight to examine your hair to see if it has turned white as hair has been known to turn upon sudden fears.

In the house with the aid of a lamp and flashlights, we examined every nook and cranny with great care, looking for wires or other possible mechanical or electrical contraptions. We looked at the bed that the force ordinarily strips and we searched high and low for something amiss, but everything was just so.

Then we latched the door leading from the sitting room, where the séance was to be held, to the bedroom – the only door leading to the little room – by means of an old fashion hook. Then we drew the shades, extinguished the oil lamp and sat talking and joking in the inky blackness that filled the room. Only the white shirts of the men, who had all doffed their coats, were visible, and those only at close range.

I was skeptical as I sat there between the two men, endowed so mysteriously. I was bored when nothing happened for a quarter of an hour. I was almost asleep *when someone called for silence. Everybody stopped talking except Mr. Markham, who kept up a steady monologue for some time.*

"Invisible Force," Mr. Burroughs said, addressing nothing in particular, "if you are here make known your presence by giving us one rap."

A rap, faint but distinct floated up from somewhere, but no one paid much attention because the rap was so faint, but we sat still for a few minutes. A picture rattled and I distinctly felt a cold blast of air on my perspiring cheek. My heart jumped a little, and all was quiet again. I figured it was all just my imagination stirred to action by the tales I had heard and the black atmosphere. But I was wide awake and not in the least bored any longer.

The picture went rattle-bang. The hook of the door, not eight inches from my head, scraped loose. The door flew open; my heart stopped beating momentarily and pounded rapidly as if trying to keep up with my rapidly retreating bravery which had vanished pronto and headlong, hand in hand with my skepticism. They were gone and there I sat trembling like an aspen leaf. But everything was quiet and my hair, which I am sure stood up for a moment, dropped back into place.

The reporter and the others took a break for a glass of water, then returned to the sitting room. His story continues.

I moved to the other side of the room then sat very close to Mr. Stone, close enough to observe any movement that might be made by his white-clad arms, and I watched closely.

As I was watching something grabbed my chair and the chairs of the two or three others near me, including the seats of Mr. Burroughs and Mr. Stone, and tossed them helter-skelter pell-mell into a heap in the center of the room. Sparks flew from the pipe of Mr. Stone held in his hand and nothing but a mass of human legs and arms, intermingled with the legs of chairs, was visible when flashlights were turned on the center of the uproar immediately after the terrific crash.

We were hardly settled after this melee when I was sitting there, watching for any outward movement on the part of the principles when I heard a faint rasping on the wall eight or nine feet to my right, high on the wall above the seat of Mr. Burroughs. Then I got another thrill of tremendous potentiality. I was holding to Mr. Stone's two thumbs with my right hand, to keep tab on his movements or to prevent him from moving. Something like a piece of tissue paper floated down into my lap and rested lightly upon the upturned tips of the fingers of my left hand.

I raised the hand and the weight became greater; then, in less than one-thousandth of the time it takes to tell it, I had tossed the picture to the middle of the floor, as lights were turned on, and trembling again in every muscle, yelled at the top of my voice, saying things perhaps that should not have been voiced anywhere, particularly not in the presence of women. Then I dashed for the open air.

When I got back after that one, we sat still for a few minutes. The hook on the door sprang upward again. The door opened gently for the first few inches and then was jerked open to its fullest width. Strangely, I was not afraid now.

Then Mr. Stone's hand moved down by his side and backward toward the bed that is often stripped. Like a cat upon a mouse, I pounced upon the wandering hand. There was nothing in it except a pipe and my solution of mystery vanished when the bed covering came tumbling through the door to fall on my arms that were still holding Mr. Stone's hand, and that was the last of the excitement.

"Invisible Force, you lazy scoundrel," Mr. Burroughs said, "Are you going to do anything else tonight? If so, rap once." The Invisible Force, evidently a very temperamental and lazy sort of spirit, if spirit it be, didn't answer. After a few more futile attempts to get some response from the force or whatever it was – the party adjourned at midnight for the ride home to Norfolk.

And so it went, these unsettling sittings, most likely for the remainder of the days that the lengthy distance, their own aging, and other circumstances allowed Blind Stone and Burroughs to visit one another. Interestingly, during all of the sessions with the "Invisible Force" no one ever received any injury worse than a bump on the head. Furniture although tossed about was not reported to have been broken. Even the flying picture frames apparently were not harmed. Stone and Burroughs did not profit from their sessions, never sought publicity, and claimed not to understand what caused the strange occurrences. Although they grew more tolerant of the force, they were never really comfortable during the sessions, never able to predict what might take place. The two men who together invoked the "Invisible Force" were as baffled as their participants and onlookers as to the cause or reason for the unsettling events.

Today the former community of Sigma has been incorporated into the City of Virginia Beach but is listed on current maps as being the section along Sandbridge Road between the intersections of Flanagan's Lane to the west and New Bridge Road to the east. The little cabin is gone, but there are still residents who recall Stone and Burroughs. A former resident near that area recalled, "It was in the 1940s when I visited Henry Stone's business. I remember him as living on Sandbridge Road. He had a fish business and lived in a modest dwelling out back. Mr. Stone, although blind, could identify each person by his or her voice. His hearing was so keen that he knew who was coming by the sound of their cars. Everybody knew about Stone and Burroughs. They seemed to be remarkable men."

Poltergeists at Witchduck Point

*I look forward with great interest to the day when flying boxes,
stones, toys, heavy items of furniture, plus spontaneous fires
and water phenomena, together with the passage of matter through matter,
levitation, metal bending, to name just a few examples of
poltergeist high jinks I have personally experienced, can be explained by
electromagnetic and bioelectromagnetic activity.*

~ Maurice Grosse, 1995

n 1981, Chris Hendrix and his two roommates rented a house at the end of North Witchduck Road, where now stand relatively new homes. It was their first year of college. Two of the young men witnessed enough unexplained events in the house to give them the "willies." They were unaware of the history of the house, but swear to this day it was haunted.

Said Chris (2003), if neither Mike nor Scott was planning to be home for the evening, he would opt to stay the night with his parents in Kempsville rather than stay in the house alone. Although certain they had closed and locked up for the night, the boys heard doors slam hard enough to shake the house. On occasion they would also hear dishes rattling around in the sink, as if someone were washing them... but no one else was in the house. One time, Mike found himself locked out of his bedroom and had to enter it through a second floor window, as the bedroom door was dead bolted from the inside.

Mike moved out, leaving the other two in need of a new roommate with whom to split the rent. While in the kitchen interviewing a prospective roommate (also named Mike), Chris and Scott felt compelled to be forthright about the weird events that

187

seemed to convey with the rental. Immediately after newcomer Mike asserted with bravado what a ghost could do if he was in the house, the kitchen window for no apparent reason crashed into the sink!

It was probably in the 1990s that the house, on prime waterfront property, was razed and replaced with one of the larger, lovely homes on the point. The owners of the new house have reported no such strange happenings. Perhaps the poltergeist, if that's what it was, has moved on.

Prior to its development as an upscale Virginia Beach neighborhood, the area was the site of a 25-acre tract called Delhaven Nursery and Gardens, a popular showplace known in its day for the spectacular foliage on its grounds (Parker, 2003). Around 1960, Bailey Parker, Jr. bought the vacated nursery and gardens and built his and his parents' homes on the site. He also restored and rented the over 100-year-old "manor" on the site, which may have been one and the same as the house in which Hendrix and his buddies lived. Before developing the area to the neighborhood it is today, Parker and his wife raised their children and their horses for a period of about twenty years (Crist, 1968).

Phyllis and Phil

One seeing is worth a hundred tellings.

~ Chinese Proverb

he following case of an unusual companionship was found in a past Halloween issue of *The Beacon* (Giametta, 1984). Charles Thomas Cayce, grandson of the famous psychic Edgar Cayce and later Executive Director of the Association for Research and Enlightenment (A.R.E.), then specialized in child psychology and often worked with psychic children. Apparently, a Virginia Beach teenage girl named Phyllis once came to his attention as, much to her teacher's and parents' concern, she was claiming an imaginary friend. Said the girl, her invisible friend "Phil" (no kidding) sported a blonde crew cut ... and had died suddenly. Phyllis, much beyond the age when imaginary friends are age-appropriate, reported that her companion was with her all the time. She further maintained that he would only communicate with her, and only by writing on her knee.

Cayce was skeptical and decided to run a few tests. First, he opened an 800-page dictionary and asked Phyllis to ask Phil what page was open. Phil "wrote" the page number on Phyllis' kneecap ... and it was right. In fact, Phil was right twelve out of a dozen times. Cayce then opened the book and, without looking at the page number himself, asked the same of Phyllis-via-Phil. Again, the "team" was unfailingly correct.

Cayce did not conclude whether the girl was merely psychic or if she did, indeed, have a ghostly companion. Phyllis eventually lost touch with Phil: not uncommon, said Cayce, when teenagers face strong desires to conform.

Chapter 9

Events

&

Attractions

I have no faith in ghosts, according to the old sense
of the word, and I could grope with comfort
through any amount of dark old rooms,
or midnight aisles, or over church-yards,
between sunset and cock-crow. I can face a spectre.

~ Harper's New Monthly Magazine, 1852

Annual Witch Ducking

The scene was still and lonely – oozy banks skirted with pines,
and lugubrious cypresses shining in the sun, white-winged sea-fowl
flitting and screaming, the far lines of the Chesapeake coast,
and the dim haze toward the shore of the Atlantic.
On the banks are the crowd of people who have come to witness ...
and the sheriff and his posse are ready to carry out the order of the court.
... And so the test begins.

~ John Esten Cooke, 1884

Since 2001, the public has been invited to participate in sponsored trips to the telling or reenactment of Grace Sherwood's trial-by-water ducking that took place on July 10, 1706. The destination is the deep, dark water of the Lynnhaven River off Witchduck Point and Witchduck Bay, both named for our famous "witch." Through the research of Belinda Nash and others, the exact ducking site was located and marked. On the anniversary of Grace's ducking, kayakers and canoeists are escorted either to the marker or to a designated location more visible to those spectators who wish to remain on shore. In the same waters that set the scene for the actual witch-ducking trial, a cast portraying Grace Sherwood, court members, and the jury tells the whole story through scripts and details exactly as church records stated so long ago. In 2006, the event featured a land reenactment of the trial preceding the ducking as well as Grace's ultimate exoneration.

Also annually on July 10th, Ferry Plantation House is open to the public in celebration of Grace Sherwood Day. Visitors can view the records of Grace's twelve trials, learn about the White and Sherwood families of Pungo, as well as witness how she used her various herbs. Interpreters portray her life through poetry and ballads written in her honor. The Legend of Grace Sherwood lives on in Virginia Beach.

Contact Ferry Plantation House for details of the July 10th annual commemoration of Grace Sherwood's trial and ducking. Contact either Ferry Plantation House or Wild River Outfitters for details on reserving a spot on the boating adventure portion of the event, if a boating trip is planned. The information numbers are (757) 473-5626 and (757) 431-8566, respectively. For more information about Grace Sherwood, see page 126.

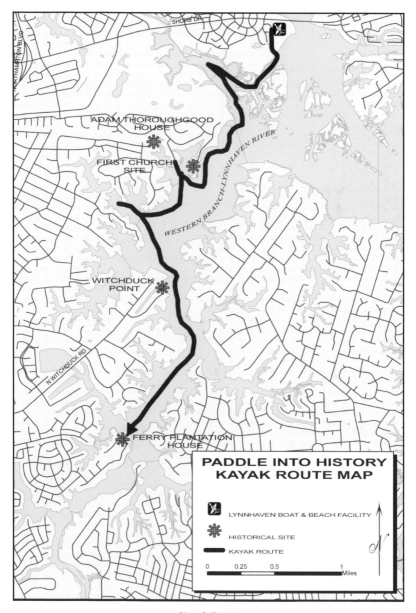

Kayak Route

Nightmare Mansion

Oh gosh, I can't see! Wait...wait...slow down! Is that a door??? Which
way do we go? I hope nothing grabs my ankles...
This is a waking nightmare...

~ Lillie Gilbert and Deni Norred, 2004

irginia Beach has a scary house of haunts called the Nightmare Mansion, located at 20th Street and Atlantic Avenue. It strives to scare. The authors can attest that the mansion is successful in its mission. At the onset of their tour, the greeters advise the brave-hearted that this is an intense event, designed for adults. "Intense to the max," is how one of the authors responded when asked afterward about her experience. Her report follows:

> *Immediately upon entering, the usher greets the guests with a gush of warnings, including, "Keep your hands to yourself for your own protection." At the top of the entry stairs, suddenly a door slams teeth-jarring-hard behind the walkers and immediately the creepiness settles in. Darkness does not beckon; in fact, it terrifies. Knowing not to put one's hands out, the guest baby-steps into the darkness. Inching slowly forward, the guest's feelings are reduced to memories of being a small child in another dark time afraid to stick even a toe over the side of the bed. Reaching tentatively with fingertips barely touching the wall, there is suddenly no way forward. "You forgot your map? Ha, ha, ha...," booms a voice in the chamber. In another moment, an eerie voice calls the guest's own name. How can this be?*
>
> *At certain times, visual clues are disorienting, as is the sense of direction. A hall of painted walls is further distorted by a flashing strobe. The mind senses nothing as*

*it should be and is on red alert. Loud abrupt noises and
unexpected happenings add to the mystery.*

Beach local Chrissie Harney (2004) remembers going to this
establishment on Atlantic that offers chills and thrills. "I was never
really scared, but my friends were. Scared big time! The thing I
remember the most was something like jail bars at the end of the visit.
You touched them and they sparked. I never got over that." While
sparks are no longer part of the event, there are plenty of chills to be
had. Wait 'til you see what's behind those bars now! For admission fees
and information, call (757) 428-3327. That's 428-FEAR. Visit their
website at youwillscream.com.

The Business of Scaring People

Have you ever thought about what it might be like to be in
the business of scaring people? Many ushers/actors in the
commercial haunted house industry take great pride and
pleasure in their duties. Ryan Moore (2004), previously of
Nightmare Mansion, offered the following about his obligations:

*A commercial haunted house's purpose is to present an
atmosphere of danger to the patron while simultaneously
presenting them with no real harm. At our establishment, we
use an original method to achieve this. Rather than the expected,
"Boo: I'm a scary ghost and I'm going to kill you," we strive
for more of a personal scare, something that gets the customer
thinking. The best weapon we have is the customer's mind. I
personally like to describe it as a walk through an old mental
asylum where all the patients have escaped their confines. I
was in the haunted house business for approximately four
years and have come to realize this is the best method.*

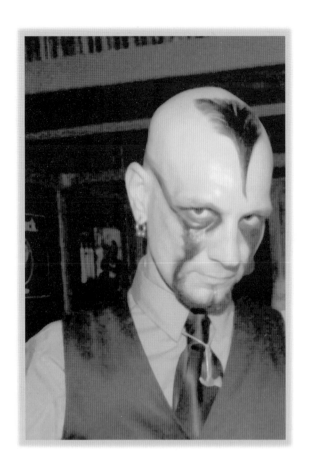

Hunt Club Farm's
Haunted Halloween Fest

So spake the grisly Terror.

~ John Milton, *Paradise Lost*

 ach October since 1988, thrill seekers have found freakish fun at Hunt Club Farm's Haunted Halloween Fest. The bravest board the Haunted Hayride wagon, an annual attraction that tours spooky surroundings staffed by dozens of actors posing as vampires, ghouls, serial killers, and their victims. Special effects make a walk through "The Village of the Dead" cemetery a downright hair-raising experience. Some years, nightfall turns a cornfield maze into the Field of Screams, in which is hidden the infamous psychotic farmer with his cleaver. "Mr. Vogel," as he is called, is named after (but bears no resemblance to, by looks or by nature) Hunt Club's now-deceased former owner, John C. Vogel (1924 – 2003). To appeal to differing ages, the Fall Festival offers more benign activities for the younger, impressionable set, including a petting barn and pumpkin patch.

The Vogels have owned and operated the 30-acre farm on London Bridge Road since the 1960s. J. D. Vogel and his wife Randi carry on the traditional fall festival at Hunt Club Farm, 2388 London Bridge Road. Call (757) 427-9520 or visit them on the web at www.huntclubfarm.com.

Chapter 10

Resources

Everything that relates, whether closely or more distantly, to psychic phenomena and to the action of psychic forces in general, should be studied just like any other science. There is nothing miraculous or supernatural in them, nothing that should engender or keep alive superstition.

~ Alexandra David-Neel,
Magic and Mystery in Tibet, 1932

Association for Research and Enlightenment: A.R.E.

Nothing in life is to be feared. It is only to be understood.

~ Marie Curie

I n cases of a paranormal, spiritual, or otherworldly nature, the services of the Association for Research and Enlightenment (A.R.E.) are often called upon. A.R.E., founded in 1931, is a global network of people who offer conferences, educational activities, and information based on concepts and ideas found in the work of Edgar Cayce. The collected readings of Cayce, the well-known psychic (1877-1945), also known as "The Sleeping Prophet," were housed in the original building built at the oceanfront in 1920. Today's facility, which includes a library and educational center, is headquarters for Edgar Cayce Centers in over twenty-five countries. The local complex is at 67th Street and Atlantic Avenue, Virginia Beach, Virginia (23451). Call (757) 428-3588 for more information. The website is www.edgarcayce.org.

The Center for Paranormal Research & Investigation

In search of the truth through perseverance …

~ former Virginia Ghosts & Hauntings Research Society website, 2004

his group is comprised of an interesting collection of professional people from all walks of life. The founder of the group, Bobbie Atristain, will quickly explain that while they believe in the paranormal, they will investigate using rigorous standards, the scientific method, as well as an introductory set of no less than 75 questions for the inhabitants of the building under investigation (Atristain, 2004). They never jump to conclusions about an alleged haunting or paranormal event until they have exhausted all normal or natural explanations, a process which can take many hours or days. They utilize many types of sophisticated equipment to record data and always have back-ups for their gear, observations, and experiences. It is unusual for a single investigator to conduct an on-site survey.

One investigator with the Virginia Beach pod is Gabriel Stempinski, a trained physicist. He states that many times people will try to fool the investigators and he has some fool-proof systems that the group employs to prevent hoaxes. He always approaches the house or building under study with the mindset that nothing is abnormal. He and his group members will be totally objective and use many different mediums to record activity. The quote they are fond of is, "Ghost hunting is hours of boredom and seconds of panic" (Stempinski, 2004).

When asked about an "unboring" event that was totally unexplainable through all of the rigorous testing, Gabriel cited many. One particularly memorable example he offered was the implosion of a television screen while in a "haunted" house.

One of the authors attended the *Southeastern Virginia Paranormal Seminar* in Virginia Beach, Virginia in April of 2004 and came away with the understanding that this group of researchers is adamant about fact-finding to explain away what is reported to them to be abnormal and unusual. They always approach the unknown with a combination of respect and curiosity, hoping to find answers for the unexplained. Their by-line on the flyer for the 2004 seminar sums up their quest: "Those who continue to search will find answers, and undoubtedly more questions."

For more information about the group, contact them at www.virginiaghosts.com.

Science and Reason in Hampton Roads

Extraordinary claims require extraordinary evidence.

~ Carl Sagan

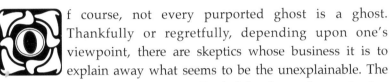f course, not every purported ghost is a ghost. Thankfully or regretfully, depending upon one's viewpoint, there are skeptics whose business it is to explain away what seems to be the unexplainable. The local *Science and Reason in Hampton Roads* "ghostbuster" organization (SRHR), founded in 2000, is a group of scientists and other interested folks that takes on the task of investigating "modern pseudoscience." In the following case, a potential haunting of a Virginia Beach home was brought to the attention of SRHR (Weinstein, 2001; Ruehlmann, 2001).

A Virginia Beach couple called "George" and "Mary" (not their real names) sought help about the eerie events they were experiencing in their new home, graphically described by a neighbor as the site of not only a murder but also the tragic death of a child taken by cancer. The couple had been frightened by a door that had slammed by itself, a bright form that had moved across the kitchen at night, and the fervently swaying blinds of their bedroom window. Additionally, Mary had heard the giggling of a child at the foot of the bed. Such events so rattled her that she became afraid to even undress in her home, as she felt constantly "watched."

Beside herself, Mary attempted to call the parapsychology department of Old Dominion University to ask for help. While there is no parapsychology department at ODU, the call she placed was timely as the newly formed local organization Science and Reason in Hampton Roads (SRHR) was just getting under way. Dr. Larry Weinstein, co-founder of the club, took the call. Even timelier for George and Mary, Dr. Joe Nickell, a Senior Fellow of the Committee for the Scientific Investigation of Claims of the Paranormal (CSICOP), was in town to help organize SRHR. Nickell had the investigation of numerous "haunted" houses under his belt. He agreed to make a house call.

Nickell and the two founders of SRHR, Larry Weinstein and Sandy Brenner, paid a visit to the Virginia Beach house. After the three modern-day ghostbusters listened to the couple and investigated the premises, Nickell suggested possible physical causes for the described events. For instance, the interplay of the air conditioner and an open fireplace flue may have accounted for pressure changes that would make a door slam. Headlights shining on the kitchen wall could account for the moving light in the kitchen, and the draft of lifted bedcovers could have caused the bedroom blinds to shake. He explained to George and Mary the unreliability of peripheral vision and the "limitations of human perception," how a tired brain can lead to misinterpretations of what one sees and hears.

Ghosts are the pests of science. Plausible reasons for the unsettling events at George and Mary's house have been given. One lingering question remains: what or who was the giggling girl? We can always hope that not all of our perceptions can be explained by science.

Science and Reason in Hampton Roads (SRHR) is an organization devoted to the critical examination of dubious or extraordinary claims. For more information about the organization *Science and Reason in Hampton Roads* (SRHR), one can visit their website at: http://www.srhr.wetpaint.com.

Ghost F.I.R.E. Haunts

'Tis true; 'tis certain; man though dead retains Part of himself;
the immortal mind remains.

~ Homer

ounded by Miss Teddy Skyler in 2007, Ghost F.I.R.E. Haunts is a small private group of paranormal investigators who not only investigate, but intervene on behalf of those in the local community and most of the East Coast who are victims of what they suspect to be hauntings. The team incorporates investigative equipment, instinct, education, and eye witness testimony to fully investigate each claim or concern. They then follow through with a plan to resolve the situation/haunting, when possible. The "F.I.R.E." in the group's title formerly stood for Forensic Investigation, Research, and Education. To address their mission of education, Teddy Skyler, with the help of various other paranormal teams, organized the Eastern Paranormal Investigators Co-operative Conference (EPIC CON) in Virginia Beach in 2010. More recently, the acronym F.I.R.E. changed tracks to represent Fun Investigations Recreation and Exploration.

Ghost F.I.R.E. Haunts can be reached by e-mail at SuprTeddy@aol.com.

References

1920 and 1930 Federal Census Schedules

"Acute Distress In Wash Woods Checked By Red Cross Chapter," February 28, 1936. *Virginia Beach News*. Virginia Beach, VA: Princess Anne Printing and Publishing, Inc.

"Andy" and "Hannah." Personal communication, July 17, 2004.

Ashley, Joan. September 18, 1977. "Things Go Bump in the Night – And Worse." *The Beacon*. Norfolk, VA: Landmark Communications.

Atristain, Bobbie. Personal communication, 2004.

Bailey, Parker Jr. Personal communication, September 28, 2003.

Barden, Thomas (editor). 1992. *Virginia Folk Legends*. Charlottesville, VA: University Press of Virginia.

Barnas, Cameron. Personal communication, February 11, 2004.

Barrow, Mary Reid. October 31, 1993. "A psychic twosome pals from childhood." *The Beacon*. Norfolk, VA: Landmark Communications.

————. April 23, 1995. "Venerable cottage being spared for a new life as a restaurant." *The Beacon*. Norfolk, VA: Landmark Communications.

————. June 15, 1997. "Old-fashioned house is tucked away in modern neighborhood." *The Beacon*. Norfolk, VA: Landmark Communications.

————. December 12, 2002. "Uprooting Rose Hall." *The Beacon*. Norfolk, VA: Landmark Communications.

Baum, Dan. 2001, *Citizen Coors: A Grand Family Saga of Business, Politics, and Beer*. New York, NY: Harper Collins Publishers, Inc.

Belanga, Marshall. Personal communication, July 18, 2004.

Bennett, Robert F. 1998. *Sand Pounders*. Washington, DC: US Coast Guard Historian's Office, US Coast Guard Headquarters.

Berry, Deborah. Personal communication, March 19, 2010.

Berson, Pat. Personal communication, February 16, 2004.

Bonko, Larry. November 30, 1973. "Larry Bonko." *The Ledger-Star*. Norfolk, VA: Norfolk-Portsmouth Newspapers, Inc.

Brown, Alexander Crosby. 1974. *Chesapeake Landfalls*. Chesapeake, VA: Norfolk County Historical Society of Chesapeake.

Brown, Catherine Barnett. Personal communication, July 27, 2004.

Buffington, Ann Winslow. Personal communication, August 12, 2004.

Buffington, Emily. Personal communication, December, 1986.

Burroughs, E.W. 1953. *The Invisible Forces*, Virginia Beach, VA: self-published.

Campbell, Charles. 1860. *History of the Colony and Ancient Dominion of Virginia*. Philadelphia, PA: J.B. Lippincott & Company.

Capwell, Phyllis M. Personal communication, June 5, July 16, 2004.

Carlson, Tina & Juliano, Dave. "Haunted Places in Virginia," *The Shadowlands*, 2002. http://theshadowlands.net/.

Castleberry, Amy. April 5, 2003. "Bulldozer is razing a piece of Beach history." *Virginian-Pilot*. Norfolk, VA: Landmark Communications.

Charlene. Personal Communication, July 23, 2010.

Corby, Mary Beth. Personal communication, March 19, 2004.

Creecy, John Harvie, editor. 1954, Virginia Antiquary, Volume 1: Princess Anne County Loose Papers, 1700-1789, Richmond, VA: The Dietz Press, Inc.

Crist, Helen. July 26, 1968. "Beach Showplace Still Has Charm, Beauty, Warmth." *The Beacon*. Norfolk, VA: Landmark Communications.

Crist, Helen. May 4, 1972. "Wishart House Was Home To Them Many Years Ago." *Virginia Beach Sun*. Virginia Beach, VA: Byerly Publications.

Death Notices. June 6, 1929. *The New York Times*. New York, NY: The New York Times Company.

Dinsmore, Christopher. January 27, 2001. "73-year-old landmark Beach restaurant razed." *The Virginian-Pilot*. Norfolk, VA: Landmark Communications.

Dougherty, Kerry. November 1, 1990. "Ghosts play disappearing act." *The Beacon*. Norfolk, VA: Landmark Communications.

Dunphy, Janet. October 9, 2003. "City takes possession of Thoroughgood House." *The Beacon*. Norfolk, VA: Landmark Publications, Inc.

"Ellen." Personal communication, Spring, 2004.

Eller, E.M. 1931. *The Foreshore of Virginia*. Norfolk, VA: Eugene L. Graves, Inc.

Evans-Hylton, Patrick. July 31, 2003. "A century by the sea." *The Beacon*. Norfolk, VA: Landmark Communications.

False Cape State Park Guide. Virginia State Parks.

Fentress, Dan. Personal communication, July 31, 2003.

File Box # 517, Princess Anne County Courthouse, VA, in folder of Justice of Peace Warrants, 1924. Richmond, VA: Virginia State Library.

Ford, Marlene. September 23, 1994. "Civic League mulls Ferry Farm ghost." *The Beacon*. Norfolk, VA: Landmark Communications.

Foss, William O. 2002. *The Norwegian Lady and the Wreck of the Dictator*. Revised Edition. Virginia Beach, VA: Noreg Books.

Gambrell, Bill. Personal communication, March 19, 2004.

Giametta, Charles. October 30/31, 1984. "Strange but True." *The Beacon*. Norfolk, VA: Landmark Communications.

Gooding, Mike. May 26, 1982. "Fields, West, Presley, Wayne Attend Opening: House of Wax Features Horror, History, Fame." *Virginia Beach Sun*. Virginia Beach, VA: Byerly Publications.

Graziadei, Jim. Personal communication, August 4, 2004.

Graziadei, Juanita. Personal communication, August 10, 2003.

Grube, Martin. 1994. *The Virginia Beach Fire Department: A Pictorial History 1907-1994*. Winston-Salem, NC: Jostens Printing and Publishing.

Harney, Chrissie. Personal communication, February 18, 2004.

Harrell, Jerry. Personal communication, October 6, 2003.

Hendrix, Chris. Personal communication, August 24, 2003.

Herbert, David. Personal communication, November 2003.

Herbert, Elizabeth. Personal communication, November 6, 2003.

Herbert, Page. Personal communication, November 5, 2003.

Herron, Stephanie. Personal communication, May 21, 2003.

Hissem, Steve. "Hissem in America," *The Hissem-Montague Family*. http://balder.prohosting.com/shissem/Hissem_In_America.html.

Holzer, Hans. 1997. *Ghosts: True Encounters with the World Beyond*. New York, NY: Black Dog & Leventhal Publishers.

Hood, Charlene. Personal communication, March 19, 2010.

Hugo, Nancy Ross and Kirwan, Jeff. 2008. *Remarkable Trees of Virginia*. Earlysville, VA: Albemarle Books.

Johnson, Jim. Personal communication, July 21, 2004.

Joyner, William. Personal communication, June, 2004.

Keeling, John W. Personal communication, November, 2002.

Kellam, Sadie and Kellam, V. Hope. 1958. *Old Houses in Princess Anne*

Virginia. Portsmouth, VA: Printcraft Press, Inc.

Kyle, Louisa Venable. 1969. *The History of Eastern Shore Chapel and Lynnhaven Parish*. Norfolk, VA: Teagle and Little, Inc.

Kyle, Louisa Venable. 1973. *The Witch of Pungo*. Virginia Beach, VA: Four O'Clock Farms Publishing Company.

Lacey, Elton and Bonnie. "The Legend of Thomas Lacy and the Pirate," *Welcome to the Web Links of Elton and Bonnie Lacey*, http://homepages.rootsweb.com/~elacey/.

McDevitt, James. May 18, 1967. "Adam Should See His Home Now," *The Beacon*, Norfolk, VA: Norfolk-Portsmouth Newspapers, Inc.

Mahan, Lawrence, "Figureheads and Other Whimsical Carvings," *Schooner Larinda*, 2000. http://www.larinda.com/figurehead.html.

Mansfield, Stephen S. 1989. *Princess Anne County and Virginia Beach: a Pictorial History*. Virginia Beach, VA: The Donning Company/Publishers.

Martin, Carl. Personal communication, May, 2005.

McAtamney, Patrick. Personal communication, December 14, 2003.

McElhaney, Robin. Personal communication, August 10, 2003.

McFall, Sandy. Personal communication, August 6, 2003.

Merriam Webster's Collegiate Dictionary, 10th ed., s.v. "tunnel."

Mitchell, Bradley. Personal communication, February 11, 2004.

Mizal-Archer, Michelle. April 1, 2003. "Fight continues to save Beach home." *Virginian-Pilot*. Norfolk, VA: Landmark Communications.

Moore, D. 2001. "A General History of Blackbeard the Pirate, the *Queen Anne's Revenge* and the *Adventure*."

Moore, Ryan. Personal communication, June, 2004.

Moreland, Jimmy. 1998. *The Witch of Pungo: the Story of Grace Sherwood.* Self-published.

Muller, Caroline. Personal communication, July 23, 2010.

Nash, Belinda. Personal communication, June 2004.

Neal, Misty. Personal communication.

Norfolk Museum Bulletin. March, 1961. "Thoroughgood House Gift." Norfolk, VA: The Norfolk Museum.

Nugent, Nell Marion. 1992. *Cavaliers and Pioneers, Abstracts of Virginia Land Patents and Grants, Volume I, 1623-1666.* Richmond, VA: Virginia State Library.

Obituaries. June 6, 1929. *The Virginian-Pilot.* Norfolk, VA: Virginian and Pilot Publishing Company.

Obituaries. September 16, 1997. *The Virginian-Pilot.* Norfolk, VA: Landmark Communications.

O'Connor, Larry. September 29/30, 1987. "It's alive?! No, it's wax." *The Beacon.* Norfolk, VA: Landmark Communications.

Pouliot, Richard & Julie. 1986. *Shipwrecks on the Virginia Coast and the Men of the Life-Saving Service.* Centreville, MD: Tidewater Publishers.

Princess Anne County Deed Book 47, p. 519.

Rain, Mary Summer. 1993. *Phantoms Afoot: Helping the Spirits Among Us.* Norfolk, VA: Hampton Roads Publishing Company, Inc.

Rangel, Craig: Consumer Information Sr. Representative, Coors. Personal communication, August 7, 2003.

Reed, Jane. Personal communication, April 3, 2004.

Reid, Brenda. Personal communication, November 21, 2003.

Roberts, Gerald Anthony. Personal communication, August 2003.

Romano, Rick. Personal communication, July 9, 2004.

Ruehlmann, William. June 24, 1981. "Queen of the Beach: Grand old Cavalier Hotel gets a facelift." *The Ledger-Star*. Norfolk, VA: Norfolk-Portsmouth Newspapers, Inc.

Ruehlmann, William. May 27, 2003. "Smashing Atoms, Mirrors, and Superstitions," *Port Folio Weekly*. Norfolk, VA: Landmark Communications.

Ruegsegger, Bob. October 30, 2003. "Making Contact." *The Beacon*. Norfolk, VA: Landmark Communications.

Rutherford, Laine. April 4, 2002. "Oh, the stories she can tell." *The Beacon*. Norfolk, VA: Landmark Communications.

Scott, Susie. Personal communication, August, 2003.

Shanks, Ralph and York, Wick; York, Lisa, ed. 1996. *The U.S. Life-Saving Service: Heroes, Rescues and Architecture of the Early Coast Guard*. Petaluma, CA: Costano Books.

Skyler, Teddy. Personal communication, November 11, 2011.

"Station Dam Neck Mills, Virginia," *United States Coast Guard*. February 2001, http://www.uscg.mil/hq/g%2Dcp/history/stations/dam%20neck%20mills.html.

Starr, Pam. April 11, 1997. "A curious blend: a former 19th century tavern, a church built in 1792, strip malls and fast food restaurants are all part of what make General Booth Boulevard an eclectic mix," *The Beacon*. Norfolk, VA: Landmark Communications.

Stempinski, Gabriel. Personal communication, 2004.

Stone, Martha. Personal communication, February 21, 2004.

Tagg, Larry. 1998. *The Generals of Gettysburg: The Leaders of America's Greatest Battle*. Cambridge, MA: Da Capo Press.

Taylor, L.B. Jr. 1990. *The Ghosts of Tidewater and Nearby Environs*. Self-published.

Tazewell, C.W. Jr., Editor. 1982. *Walke Family Scrapbook*. Virginia

Beach, VA: Self-published.

Tazewell, C.W., Compiler. 1991. *Family Underground: A Record of Tazewell and Allied Families Burial Plots*. Virginia Beach, VA: W.S. Dawson Co.

The Cavalier. 2002. http://www.cavalierhotel.com.

Tuttle, David. Personal communication, August 5, 2003.

"Two-Mile Tree." May, 1931, *Virginian-Pilot & the Norfolk Landmark*. Norfolk, VA: G. and G. Corporation.

Turner, Florence Kimberly. 1984. *Gateway to the New World: A History of Princess Anne County, Virginia 1607-1824*. Early, SC: Southern Historical Press, Inc.

Tyler, Fielding. Personal communication, February 8, 2004.

United States War Department, United States Record and Pension Office, United States War Records Office, et al. 1884. *The war of the rebellion: a compilation of the official records of the Union and Confederate armies*. Series 1 - Volume 11 (Part II). Washington, D.C.: Government Printing Office.

Virginia Beach Public Library. 1996. *The Beach*. Virginia Beach, VA: Department of Public Libraries, City of Virginia Beach.

"Virginia Beach, VA History, 1999-2003," *Williamsburg, VA: Vacation-Creations.Com*. http://www.virginiabeachon-line.com.

Vojtech, Pat. 1996. *Lighting the Bay*. Centreville, MD: Tidewater Publishers.

Wacker, Debi. August 17, 2003. "Jack and Jill will find elegance On the Hill." *The Beacon*. Norfolk, VA: Landmark Communications.

Wagner, Janet. Personal communication, May, 2006.

Warren, Nancy. Personal communication, February 16, 2004.

"Wealthy Colorado manufacturer, 82, is killed in fall," June 6, 1929. *Virginian-Pilot*. Norfolk, VA: Virginian and Pilot Publishing Company.

Weinstein, Larry. Spring 2001. "The Visit," *Catalyst Magazine*. Norfolk, VA: Old Dominion University.

Whichard, Rogers Dey. 1959. *The History of Lower Tidewater Virginia*. New York, NY: Lewis Historical Publishing Company, Inc.

Whitehurst-Buffington Foundation. P.O. Box 56114, Virginia Beach, VA 23456, 2012.

"William Thomas Butt Dead from Hurricane Injury; Damage Cited." September 25, 1936. *Virginia Beach News*. Virginia Beach, VA: Princess Anne Printing and Publishing Company, Inc., .

Workman, Leslie Mann. Personal communication, January 2, 2003; November 14, 2003.

Yarsinske, Amy. 2002. *Virginia Beach: A History of Virginia's Golden Shore*. Charleston, SC: Arcadia Publishing.

List of Illustrations

Notes

Notes

Notes

Notes

Notes

Notes

About the Authors

Lillie Gilbert has been a Virginia Beach, Virginia resident since 1967. She received a BA in English Literature from Queens College and an MA from the College of William and Mary. Lillie taught for 17 years in the Virginia Beach City Public Schools and was owner of Wild River Outfitters for 32 years. Actively involved in environmental affairs, Lillie serves as a volunteer for the Virginia Beach Department of Parks and Recreation, Lynnhaven River NOW and Clean the Bay Day events. A life member of the Princess Anne County/ Virginia Beach Historical Society, Lillie is also a member of the Virginia Outdoor Writers Association, The Old Coast Guard Station, Friends of Ferry Plantation House, Virginia Historical Society and National Historical Trust.

Belinda Nash is a Canadian who moved to Virginia Beach, Virginia in the early 1980s. Intrigued by the history of this area, local folklore has become dear to her. While doing research, inconsistencies in local history revealed that more research was necessary, especially on Grace Sherwood, The Witch of Pungo. Belinda interprets the life and times of Grace Sherwood at Virginia Beach's historic Ferry Plantation House, local schools, and various civic events. She is a member of the Princess Anne County/ Virginia Beach Historical Society, one of the Board of Directors of Ferry Plantation House, treasurer of Pembroke Meadows/ Shores Civic League Association, and historian at Old Donation Church.

Deni Norred has resided in Virginia Beach, VA since 1988. She received a teaching degree in Special Education from James Madison University and an Educational Specialist degree in School Psychology from Radford University. Deni taught three years in southwest Virginia and was a School Psychologist in Bedford County, VA and Newton County, GA prior to employment with Virginia Beach schools in 1988, where she continues to practice. Deni is a member of the Princess Anne County/Virginia Beach Historical Society, Friends of Ferry Plantation House, and The Old Coast Guard Station. She occasionally contributes articles to various newsletters and enjoys speaking to civic groups on topics of local history and lore.